ABOUT THE AUTHOR

Malachy says:

'I do a lot of wandering about, looking for stories. One day, in a graveyard, I found a badge, with a weird message on it and a website address. I couldn't track down the website, or work out what the message meant, but it got me thinking some pretty weird thoughts, and this book is the result.

'In Ireland, where I come from, if someone calls you an amadan, it means you're a fool. I'm not sure why, really, because amadans are fairly clever, as far as I can tell. And if you ever get to meet one, on a soft summer night, don't call him a fool or you'll be sure to regret it.'

Malachy lives in Wales, in a big old house overlooking the Irish Sea, with his wife, Liz, and assorted cats, bats and woodlice. He writes for all ages, from pop-up books to teenage novels. You can find out more about him by looking at his website: www.malachydoyle.co.uk

D1148586

CONTENTS

for Liz

ORCHARD BOOKS
96 Leonard Street, London EC2A 4XD
Orchard Books Australia
32/45-51 Huntley Street, Alexandria, NSW 2015
ISBN 1 84362 612 8
First published in Great Britain in 2004
A paperback original
Text © Malachy Doyle 2004
The right of Malachy Doyle to be identified as the author
of this work has been asserted by him in accordance
with the Copyright, Designs and Patents Act, 1988.
A CIP catalogue record for this book is available from the British Library.
1 3 5 7 9 10 8 6 4 2 (hardback)
1 3 5 7 9 10 8 6 4 2 (paperback)
Printed in Great Britain

Amadans

MALACHY DOYLE

ORCHARD BOOKS

1
THEY'RE COMING TO GET YOU

'I spy money!' cried Jimmy MacIver, running to pick up the silvery shiny thing lying on the pavement.

But it wasn't money. It was a badge. And on it were the words: 'AmadansAnonymous. Comingtogetyou.'

It didn't make a lot of sense to Jimmy. But he pinned it on to his T-shirt anyway, because that's what you do with badges. And off he went.

'What's an amadan, Dad?' he said, when he got home.

'No idea, son,' said his dad, busy wrestling with the Hoover. It looked like the Hoover was winning.

But the old man in the corner looked up from his porridge. 'What was that you said, our Jimmy?'

'An amadan, Grandad. Any idea what it is?'

Grandad's face went grey. Well, it was grey already, to tell you the truth. Grey and pointy, with wispy bits of white sticking out of his nose and ears and mostly his chin. But suddenly it turned a whole heap greyer.

'Amadans – stay well clear of them fellows!' he wheezed.

'Why?' asked Jimmy, surprised. 'Who are they? What do they do?'

But Grandad buried his head back in his porridge and that was that. There was no point hoping for more out of him, as Jimmy well knew. Two sentences a day was the most you ever got out of Dad's old dad since his pet budgie died.

Jimmy got the dictionary down off the top shelf. First he checked 'anonymous'.

'Of unknown name,' it said.

'That's a lot of help,' he muttered. 'I'm looking for an unknown thingy with an unknown name.'

Then he looked up 'amadan'. First he found 'amadavat'.

'A small Indian songbird,' said Jimmy to himself. 'Maybe that's what Grandad's poor dead budgie was. Maybe that's why he went a greyer shade of grey when I mentioned it.' But he didn't think so, not really.

Then he found 'amadou', which the book said meant 'tinder from fungi'. He had to look up 'tinder' and 'fungi', for that's the trouble with using dictionaries – once you start, you never know where to stop. Burning mushrooms, it seemed to mean. Sounds like Dad's cooking, thought Jimmy.

But he couldn't find amadan. Not anywhere.

Jimmy went out for a ride on his bike. But he'd only got to the corner when he heard someone yelling his name.

'Jimmy, Jimmy, stop!' It was Nita Nextdoor, all curls and urgency.

'What's up, Nita?'

'I've found something,' said Nita. 'Something weird. I bet you'll never guess what it is.'

'A Vietnamese pot-bellied pig?' suggested

Jimmy. 'The Lost City of Atlantis?'

'Don't be silly, Jimmy. It's in my pocket.'

'Pope John Paul the Twenty-third? A nuclear submarine?'

'No, it's a badge, stupid.' Nita pulled it out. 'What do you think it means?'

'AmadansAnonymous.Comingyourway,' it said.

'That's spooky. Look at this,' said Jimmy, pointing to the one on his T-shirt.

'Mine was on a bench in the park,' Nita told him. 'I asked Mum what it meant, but she hadn't a clue.'

'No one has,' said Jimmy. 'Except maybe Grandad.'

The next morning, Jimmy was busy scoffing his cereal and watching Danger Dog on the telly when Grandad looked up from his porridge.

'Beware the Stroke Lads, boy!' he roared, pointing at Jimmy. 'They'll root you to the spot, and that's that!'

'Huh?' Jimmy nearly choked on his cereal. And then he realised he was still wearing yesterday's T-shirt. And yesterday's badge. Which was what

Grandad was pointing at.

There was no answer to Jimmy's heartfelt huh, though, for there was nothing more to be said. Not by Grandad. Not today. He'd had his two sentences. Any more and he'd be over the limit.

'Grandad definitely knows something,' Jimmy told Nita, while they were waiting for the school bus. 'Only he won't say.'

'Or he can't,' said Nita, who was aware of Grandad's little problem.

At school they asked Mrs Schloss, the librarian. She knew everything about everything, and if there was anything she didn't, she knew how to find out.

'Amadan?' she said, scratching her chin. 'Rings a bell, but I can't for the life of me remember what it means. Try the Internet,' she suggested. 'There's sure to be something on there.'

So Jimmy did. He typed it in. 'A-M-A-D-A-N.'

'Wow!' he cried, as it opened up before him. 'Two thousand, one hundred and eighty-two web page matches!'

'Yeah, that's the trouble with computers,' said Nita. 'Too much information.'

'Stout Irish Music?' read Jimmy, starting from the top. Nita shook her head.

'Hebridean Fun and Laughter?'

'I shouldn't think so,' said Nita, drumming her fingers on the tabletop. 'Here, let me have a go.'

'Wait, this sounds a bit more like it – Celtic Mythology, Mythical Creatures.' Jimmy opened it up. 'An amadan,' he read, 'is a type of Irish fairy. Even a touch from one can cause instant and total paralysis.'

'Which means you can't move,' whispered Nita.

'Because of this special power,' they read together, 'they are sometimes known as the Stroke Lads. Amadans are particularly dangerous to criminals, or people who are out and about by moonlight. They are believed to be at their most mischievous in the month of June.'

'Hey, that's what Grandad called them!' exclaimed Jimmy. 'The Stroke Lads.'

'And it's June today,' added Nita, with a gasp. 'The first of the month.'

'Just when they're at their worst,' said Jimmy. 'I wouldn't want to be a cat burglar tonight.'

'No,' Nita agreed. 'You'd be turned to stone

while you're climbing back out of the window.'

'And I wouldn't want to be raiding the fridge for a midnight feast.'

'Me neither,' said Nita. 'Frozen to ice the minute you opened the door!'

The following morning, Jimmy tore open a new packet of cereal only to find another badge inside. 'AmadansAnonymous.Comingevercloser,' it said.

'Grandad!' he gasped. 'The Stroke Lads are after me!'

The old man jerked his head up from his breakfast at the sound of the dreaded words. He stared all around, eyes bulging behind his specs and a hunted, haunted look about him. And then he buried himself back in his porridge. It was a no-word day.

'I think the Stroke Lads might have got Grandad,' said Jimmy, when he met up with Nita. 'He wouldn't say a thing. Not even when I showed him this.' And he pointed to the new badge, pinned to his T-shirt.

But Nita had one too. She'd found it on her pillow when she woke up:

'AmadansAnonymous.Combyourhair!' it said.

'I've had enough of these stupid amadans, trying to scare everyone,' said Jimmy. 'I think it's about time we found out who they are and what they're up to.'

So that night, Nita and Jimmy snuck out of their next-door houses at midnight. The full moon shone brightly overhead as they padded up and down, down and up Nita's garden path.

But they were out there for twenty minutes and no one came. Not a policeman. Not a cat burglar. Not a midnight-feast fridge thief. Certainly not an amadan.

'Pretend to be a criminal, Jimmy,' whispered Nita. 'Maybe that'll do it.'

So Jimmy looked around for something to steal. He tiptoed across the soggy grass, picked up Nita's dad's favourite garden gnome and shoved it under his dressing gown. And suddenly he froze.

'What is it?' whispered Nita. 'Is there someone coming?'

Jimmy didn't speak. Or move.

'Jimmy!' cried Nita, running over and shaking him. But he didn't budge, not an inch.

The Stroke Lads had got him.

2
HERE COMES GRANDAD!

'Jimmy's grandad!' cried Nita, running into his house. 'Come quickly, we need your help!'

Somebody needs me, thought the old fellow, sitting up with a start. Somebody wants me to help them, like in the old days.

He jumped out of bed, grabbed his bowl of porridge from the bedside table (it's the first thing you need in a time of crisis. Well, it is if you're Jimmy's grandad) and raced down the stairs, hanging on for dear life to his pyjama bottoms.

'It's Jimmy,' cried Nita, leading him into her garden and pointing at her friend. 'The amadans have got him! He's frozen to the spot!'

But Jimmy was only mucking about. At the sight of Nita's terrified face, and Grandad in his pyjamas, he got a fit of the giggles, a fit of the shakes, and next thing the garden gnome had slipped from his hands and come crashing down on to his foot.

The giggles turned to yelps of pain, as Jimmy hopped around the garden, rubbing his throbbing toes.

But when poor old Grandad saw the gnome, a look of one-hundred-percent horror crossed his ageing greyness. In all the fuss of being woken up in the middle of the night, he'd forgotten to put his specs on, and without them, he was blind as a bat. So Nita's dad's favourite gnome looked just like an amadan, and a particularly ugly one at that.

'A Stroke Lad!' cried Grandad, horrified, and he took off like the clappers, over the fence and up to the safety of his bed, hooting like an owl.

The next day, on their way home from school, Jimmy and Nita were almost tripping over the badges. They were everywhere!

Outside the newsagent's there was one that said, 'AmadansAnonymous.Comics.' On the pavement in front of the garden centre Nita found another one, with the message, 'AmadansAnonymous.Compost.' Outside the Scout Hut was one that read, 'AmadansAnonymous.Compass.' And across the road from the Citizens' Advice Bureau, Jimmy spotted a fourth one, saying, 'AmadansAnonymous.Complain!'

'I get it!' cried Nita, at last. She was always the clever one, was Nextdoor Nita.

'What do you get?' said Jimmy.

'The missing link.'

'What missing link?'

'The link that links the badges.'

'What, like they're all white, with writing on?'

'That's pretty obvious, Jimmy.'

'Like they've all got pins on the back?'

'You'll have to do better than that.'

'Like they're all about amadans, then?'

'Mmmm,' said Nita, nodding. 'Go on…'

'Like they've all started saying something to do with where we find them,' Jimmy suggested, 'like comics and newsagents, compost and garden centres?'

'You're getting warmer, brainbox. But what do they all actually say?'

'Amadans...' said Jimmy.

'Yes...'

'AmadansAnonymous...'

'Carry on...'

'AmadansAnonymous.Comingtogetyou... comingyourway...comingevercloser...'

'Combyourhair...comics...' added Nita.

'Compost...compass...' continued Jimmy.

'Complain,' they both finished.

'So what's the missing link, then?' asked Nita, after a long silence. 'Haven't you got it yet?'

And Jimmy had! Suddenly he had! 'The words all start with com!' he cried. 'Amadans Anonymous dot com!' And he ran inside, into his dad's study, with Nita hot on his heels. 'Dad, Dad!' said Jimmy. 'Can we use the computer?'

'Why?' Jimmy's dad looked up from the flickering screen. 'What's the big hurry?'

'We need to look at a website. Quick!'

Dad tut-tutted, saved his writing, and went off

to get himself a coffee while Jimmy opened up the Internet.

Dot dot dot dot, dit dit dit dit, dot dot dot, beep beep beep beep beep, hisssssssssssssssssssssssssssss. Click on 'home' to find the search engine. Type in www.amadansanonymous.com. Fingers crossed.

'This page cannot be displayed.' Groan! Double groan!

'Let ME try!' cried Nita. And, with a mighty burp, the screen spluttered into life, and there in front of them was the ugliest face you've ever seen, all green and pointy like a seasick pixie, all gurning and squirming and squiddling around. You wouldn't want to look, because it made you feel like you feel when you've been reading in the car, only worse. You wouldn't want to look, and yet you couldn't take your eyes off it, because it was just so yucky.

The mouth opened wider, and this foul screech of a noise came out.

'Paralyse you! Paralyse you!' it shrieked.

Jimmy and Nita had their hands over their ears to block out the awful sound, when suddenly, to their utter horror, these long, wiry fingers, far too many for one hand, came right out of the screen and touched each of them in turn. And they froze. Like ice. Like statues. Like waxwork dummies.

But then Jimmy's grandad's porridge bowl, followed by Jimmy's grandad's specs, followed by Jimmy's grandad's bulgy eyes, appeared around the doorframe. 'What's all that yelling?' he croaked. 'What's all that horrible noise?'

'Paralyse you! Paralyse you!' squealed the amadan, stretching out towards him with its long bony fingers.

Grandad turned to run, but he crashed into the doorframe and porridge flew up and out and all over the door, the floor and all over the hysterical amadan who'd just been about to...

'Paffaluf-oo...' squelched the yucky creature. And Nita and Jimmy came, blinking, back to life, as the amadan slopped back towards the screen, dripping sticky goo as he went.

And what they heard, as they came back to their senses, amazed them all. It was Grandad, changed utterly by his triumph with the porridge from an amadan-fearing, word-deprived old man into some sort of a superhero.

Yes, there was Grandad, roaring at the departing amadan, yelling at the screen, as though old age and a dear-departed bird hadn't ever brought about a severe case of late-onset wimpishness. As though he'd never been short of words in his tens of thousands of days.

'Away and paralyse yourself, and stop bothering the likes of us!' Grandad hollered. 'Sure you're not a patch on the amadans we had in the old days, and you don't scare me, not one little bit. Away back in your box, you bletherskite, and leave us in peace!'

Three sentences! Forty-eight words in one go, which was nearly more than Grandad had spoken altogether in the whole two years since Long-Johns Ilver, his beloved budgie, fell off his perch and was gobbled by the cat.

Forty-eight words, fierce and strong, and the amadan's nasty little porridge-covered features were twisting and shrivelling as he was sucked back into the screen, squealing and hissing.

Jimmy and Nita were laughing their legs off. Because they'd won. Because dotty old Grandad had sent the amadan packing.

But he wasn't beaten yet, the creature from another world. Back inside the web, his powers had returned, so with one last show of strength, one last contorted smile, he threw his shrivelled arm back out of the screen and fastened his bony fingers round Jimmy's wrist, sinking his never-cut nails into his skin.

And it was too much for Jimmy, who was up and out of his chair and sliding towards the screen, through the piles of sticky porridge that had dripped off the amadan as he retreated.

'Help!' he screamed, and Nita grabbed him, desperately trying to hang on to her best friend in all the world. But he was slipping from her grasp, being pulled from all he knew, sucked into the screen by the cackling amadan, who was no bigger than Nita but a whole lot stronger.

And the last thing Jimmy's grandad

and Nextdoor Nita heard was Jimmy yelling, 'Help meeeeee!'

And the last thing they saw was Jimmy fading into the flickering screen, vanishing into the World Wide Web, disappearing into amadansanonymous.com.

3
BEHIND THE SCREEN

Jimmy woke up. He couldn't move his arms, couldn't move his legs, couldn't even turn his head. There was no rope, no string, no Sellotape – nothing obvious stopping him from moving. But then he remembered. The amadans. The Stroke Lads. They'd touched him, paralysed him.

In front of him, all he could see was a flat whiteness, above him, below him, stretching out on either side, and it took him a while to work out what it was – the back of the computer screen.

'Will you be good?' said a squeaky voice, and Jimmy nearly jumped out of his skin. Except he wasn't able to move.

He knew who it was, though. An amadan!

'I'll unparalyse you, if you'll be good,' said the voice.

'I'll be good,' Jimmy said. Or tried to.

And suddenly the feeling of tightness, the feeling of being tied up and unable to move, slipped away. Jimmy stretched, slowly, and then he turned round and saw a whole new world reaching out in front of him. As different to the boring ever-whiteness he'd just been looking at as you could ever imagine.

It was a world of colour. The wrong colour, by Jimmy's reckoning, but colour nevertheless. There were scarlet hills and yellow forests, blue fields and purple farmhouses, brown clouds in an orange sky. Like, but unlike, anything Jimmy had ever seen before.

And from behind a large pink rock appeared an amadan. Much the same as the other one, the one who'd got him into all this mess, only a whole lot friendlier, by the look of him. The same sort of pointy ears and pointy nose, but a lot rounder in the face and body. No sign of green on his skin. Smiley lines around his little piggy eyes and a stack of red hair on top that made him look like he was on fire.

'Bunsen Bernard, that's me,' said the smiling amadan, holding out his scraggy hand. 'Pleased to meet you.'

Jimmy looked at it. He wasn't at all sure he wanted to touch the hand of an amadan, never mind shake it, after what had happened last time, but such a look of upset crossed Bunsen Bernard's face when he saw the boy's hesitation that Jimmy thought he'd better.

'Pleased to meet you, Bernard,' he said, conjuring up a smile and shaking the bony hand, full of far too many fingers.

Now that he could see the amadan up close, all Jimmy's fear evaporated. For one thing, he realised how small they were. This one was obviously an adult, yet he was no taller than Jimmy. In fact, if you didn't count the stack of red hair on top, he was slightly smaller.

'But I thought you were supposed to be anonymous, Bernard,' said Jimmy. 'How come you're telling me your name?'

'Oh, we're only anonymous in the world of

humans,' replied the amadan, smiling back. 'We're quite happy for anyone to know who we are, now we're here. And you can call me Bun. That's what all my friends call me. I'm delighted to meet you, Jimmy MacIver,' he said, setting off up the lane, double-quick.

Jimmy followed him, double-quick. He hadn't a clue where he was, so the last thing he wanted was to be left behind.

'I'm sorry about what happened back there,' said Bun, when they got to the top of a rise. 'It wasn't meant to be like that. It's just that we're desperate.'

'Desperate for what?' asked Jimmy, gasping for breath. He hadn't quite got over the shock of being paralysed and transported to another world.

'For help,' answered Bun.

'What sort of help?'

'We're in danger of losing the touch. Of losing our powers of paralysis,' said the amadan, sadly.

'Are you now?' Jimmy raised an eyebrow, thinking of bony fingers and never-cut nails. 'Well, maybe that's not such a bad thing.'

'Of course it's a bad thing!' answered

Bun, shocked. 'Do you want the world, YOUR world, to be over-run by criminals?'

'How do you mean?' asked Jimmy.

'Well, that's what we do, silly,' said Bun. 'By day we live here, in the amadan world,' and he looked all around at the colourful land below him, 'but by night we patrol the human world, and if we see anyone up to no good, like a car thief or a bank robber, we splat them with our special powers. Paralyse them for a wee while, so they can't get up to any more badness.'

'So you're goodies, not baddies?' asked Jimmy, surprised.

'Of course we're goodies!' said Bun, shocked. 'Well, most of us are. You do get the odd one or two rogue amadans who try to use their powers the wrong way, but we're pretty good at finding out who they are and sorting them out before they can cause too much trouble. Or at least we have been up to now.'

'So what about the one that scared the pants off me and Nita, never mind my poor old grandad? The one that punctured my wrist with his nasty never-cut nails and dragged me in here?'

'Yes, like I said, I'm sorry about that,' said Bun. 'That's Dunk for you. He's always been a bit of a nutter, I'm afraid. We sent him off to evening classes to learn how to be more polite, but it doesn't seem to have worked.'

'It certainly doesn't! So was he *supposed* to kidnap me like that?'

'Not quite.'

'What do you mean, not quite?'

'Well, he was supposed to ask you and your friend, Nita, if you'd like to come and spend some time with us and help us out. We'd been keeping an eye on the both of you for a while, watching you as you went about your business, and we'd decided you were just the sort of clever, helpful humans we need. The badges we left lying about were a bit of a test, and you came through with flying colours. Congratulations!'

'Hmmm,' said Jimmy. It was nice to find someone who thought he was clever and helpful for a change. Unless they meant Nita was the clever one and he was only helpful. Which somehow seemed more likely.

'So he wasn't meant to give us all the shock of our lives, this Dunk character?'

'No, sorry,' answered Bun. He set off again, down the other side of the hill. 'He wasn't meant to do that. He's got a thing about humans, I'm afraid. Every time he sees one he tries to paralyse them. He can't seem to tell the difference between good or bad yet.'

'Hmmm.' Jimmy was chasing to keep up. 'I don't think much of that. Can I ask you something else?'

'You can.'

'How do I get back to my world?'

'Oh, you're not a prisoner, Jimmy. You can go back any time.'

'Any time?'

'Yes, any time.'

'Like now.'

'Well, yes, like now. But do you really have to?'

'I think I'd better. Nita and Dad and Grandad won't know where I've gone. They won't know if I'm even coming back.'

'Oh dear. I was supposed to take you to Alisha.'

'Who's Alisha?'

'Our leader. She's the one who was going to ask you to help us.'

'Well, I'll tell you what,' said Jimmy, who was quite enjoying his little chat. 'If everything's all right out there, I'll come back and see you. OK?'

'OK.'

They grinned at each other for a while.

'So how do I do it, then?' asked Jimmy.

'Do what?'

'Get back to the real world, of course.'

'This is the real world.'

'Not to me it isn't, Bunsen Bernard,' said Jimmy, smiling. 'Go on, tell me.'

'It's easy,' said Bun, laughing. 'You just slide through the computer screen.'

'Through the screen?'

Bun nodded.

'And can I get back the same way?

'You can. If we want you to.'

So Jimmy moved towards the vast expanse of whiteness he'd originally come through and placed his hand up against it. It didn't feel like anything at all, but his fingers disappeared. Quickly, he pulled them back out again, counted they were all present and correct, giving them a good wiggle just to check. Then he eased a foot through. And out again.

'You're right!' he said, looking back at the amadan. 'See you later, Bun.' And he pushed his head through.

4
ATTACK OF THE NETHERWORLDERS

'Jimmy!'

'Nita! Here, give me a hand.'

Nita pulled, and he landed in a heap on the floor beside her. 'What happened, Jimmy? Where did you go?'

'It's OK,' said Jimmy. 'I'm OK.' And he proceeded to tell her all about Bun, and why the amadans had dragged him through to their world.

'All that in a couple of minutes?' asked Nita, when he'd finished.

'It was much longer than a couple of minutes. I was talking to Bun for, well, ages.'

'No way, Jimmy,' insisted Nita. 'As soon as you'd gone I tried calling up the website. Eight times it was unavailable, and the ninth time it came good. It was definitely no more than five minutes.'

'That's handy, then,' said her friend, smiling. 'Because it means I can go in and out whenever I like, and no one'll miss me.'

'You're not seriously thinking of going back, are you?'

'I have to,' said Jimmy. 'They need me.'

'Take me with you, then,' she pleaded. 'I don't want you in there on your own. It's not safe.'

'I need you here,' answered Jimmy, 'in case you have to help me out again.'

'OK.' Nita gave in. 'But if you're not back in another five minutes, I'll call you up again.'

And with that, Jimmy clambered through. Nita pressed her fingers against the screen, but it was hard, solid. There was no way through. Not without the permission of the amadans.

Bun was waiting on the other side. 'You're back!'

'I'm back,' said Jimmy.

'I'm so pleased to see you again,' said Bun, and they chatted happily while he led Jimmy across a field, through a dark wood, and along a rough stony track to a castle. Past some fierce guards, and into a big hall, where a queenly-looking amadan sat.

'Jimmy MacIver!' she cried, beckoning him forward. 'Will you help us?'

'I will if I can, Miss,' said Jimmy, shrugging his shoulders.

'As Bun probably told you,' the Queen began, 'we're losing our powers. They weaken in winter but once spring comes they start getting strong again. Only this year, for some dreadful reason, many of us didn't get our strength back.'

'So you haven't been able to come to Earth to sort out the bad guys?'

'Not nearly as much as we usually do. That's why we had to fetch you.'

'And is that why you had to send that Dunk nutter to get me?' asked Jimmy.

'I'm afraid so. All our best amadans were either guarding my castle or out on badness duty. He was all we could spare.'

'So what is it you want me to do, Miss? I don't think I'd be much good at catching criminals.'

'Oh, no. That'd be much too risky, Jimmy.' The Queen smiled at him. 'What we actually want is for you to help find out what's making us lose our powers.'

'Hmmmm,' said Jimmy. 'It sounds like you need someone brainy, if it's thinking you're after. I'm not all that clever, you know. Not half as clever as my friend, Nita.'

'Any chance of getting her to join you, then?'

'Oh, I think she'd love to come,' answered Jimmy. 'But I wasn't sure I'd be able to get home without her, so I asked her to wait there.'

'You don't need to worry about that. I've appointed Bun as your Official Gatekeeper,' said the Queen, glancing over at the beaming amadan. 'As long as he's with you, there'll be no problem.'

Suddenly there was a terrible noise from outside. Queen Alisha rushed to the window, just as a large rock thumped against the metal bars.

'Don't panic!' cried Bun, diving under a table.

But the Queen marched over and hauled him out by the tail of his coat. 'Stop being such a wimp, Bernard. Get out there and defend me!'

'Do you want me to help?' asked Jimmy, as Bun

grabbed a shield and slingshot and ran round the room, before ducking back in under the tablecloth while no one was looking.

'No, no,' said the Queen. 'You're my guest, Jimmy. Stay here and keep me company while the guards send those silly boys packing.'

But the noises, crashes, bangs and yells were getting louder. 'It's only the NetherWorlders,' Alisha reassured him. 'They send a few of their younger tearaways over to lob rocks at us every now and again.'

'Why, who are they, these NetherWorlders?' asked Jimmy.

'They're a gang of amadans-gone-bad who've been exiled to the land beyond our boundaries. There's quite a few of them by now, and a whole new generation, too. Luckily, though, the older ones spend most of their time smoking puffweed and drinking elderbox, which is why they're never too much of a problem.'

'Maybe they're the ones who are taking away your powers?'

'Oh, no,' said Alisha. 'At least I don't think so. The trouble is, no one has the slightest idea how and why it's happening. That's why we brought you here, Jimmy. To add a different level of thinking. A human level.'

Suddenly a second rock, much bigger and heavier than the one before, crashed against the metal grill, sending it clanging to the floor. Queen Alisha ran to pick up the grill and wedge it back in place, but a shower of stones came flying through the gap, and Jimmy watched, horrified, as one sent her crown flying, a load more thumped into her head and shoulders, and she fell to the ground, moaning.

Jimmy ran over, and was just about to pull Alisha out of the way when he saw an ugly amadan, even uglier and greener than Dunk, staring at him from outside the window, at the top of a ladder.

'Paralyse you! Paralyse you!' shrieked the amadan, stretching out its long bony fingers and stabbing Jimmy in the arm.

And Jimmy instantly froze.

5

JOURNEY TO NETHEREDGE

Dot dot dot dot, dit dit dit dit, dot dot dot, beep beep beep beep beep, hisssssssssssssssssssssssssss. Click on 'home' to find the search engine. Type in www.amadansanonymous.com. And this time it worked! The site opened up, and there in front of Nita was a terrified Bun, pointing over towards the window.

Nita looked, and saw a female amadan, lying on the ground. Jimmy lay next to her, with four revolting-looking creatures all around him, poking and chirruping, celebrating their capture.

'Clear off!' yelled Nita, pushing her head up against the glass. 'Leave my friend alone!' Next thing, she was clambering through the screen, all teeth, curls and ferocity, and the NetherWorlders were so shocked at the sight of her that they scrambled back to their ladder and away.

'And don't come back!' Nita yelled, fiercer than a fox in a shedful of chickens. And then she turned to survey the damage.

'What a brave and clever human you are!' said a small voice, from under the table. It was Bun, crawling out to greet her.

But Nita wasn't in the mood for greetings. 'What were you doing lurking under the table while they hurt my poor Jimmy?' she demanded.

'I did what I could,' said Bun. 'It was me who opened up the SuperHighway, so you could come through and scare them away.'

'But what about Jimmy?' cried Nita, holding her friend. 'He's frozen solid!'

'Oh, it's just a case of the Stroke,' said Bun. And he went over and gently ran his hand over the boy's face. 'Unparalyse,' he whispered, until Jimmy's eyes opened.

'Nita!' cried Jimmy, blinking. 'What are you doing here?'

'Coming to the rescue, Jimmy,' said Nita. 'And it's just as well I did, too.'

'Here, give me a hand with the Queen!' cried Bun. 'I think she's badly hurt.'

Nita ran over to fetch a cushion to lay under Alisha's head, and Jimmy grabbed the tablecloth to keep her warm, while Bun ran off to fetch help.

Soon he hurried back in, followed by an ancient amadan. 'Oh dear,' tutted the healer, when she saw the state of the Queen. She pulled some strong-smelling herbs from a bag, held them under Alisha's nose, and then opened a tiny bottle and poured the contents down the injured amadan's throat. She cleaned up the wounds and then everyone helped to carry the Queen to her bedroom, where she fell back into a deep sleep.

'She's had a nasty shock,' the healer told them, 'but she'll feel a lot better in the morning. Some nasty cuts and bruises, but nothing that won't mend in a few days.'

'What's going on?' Nita hissed at Jimmy, as they

were going back down the stairs. 'What were those horrible-looking green things at the window trying to do?'

'They're young NetherWorlders,' said Jimmy, explaining as they went. 'Alisha says they often attack the castle for a bit of a laugh, only something's happened to make them more violent than usual. And that's not the only problem round here...' And he told her all about the good amadans losing their special powers.

'That's why the Queen brought us over,' he finished. 'To see if we could help them work out what's happening.'

Nita went off to do a bit of hard thinking. She found Jimmy and Bun in the kitchen a while later, eating apple pie and cream.

'I'm beginning to think the NetherWorlders might have something to do with the loss of the amadans' powers,' she said. 'The thing to do is for you and me, and Bun here, to sneak into their camp and do a bit of sleuthing. Listen in, see what we can see, and report back to Queen Alisha.'

'Fair enough,' said Jimmy, helping himself to another portion of apple pie. 'What do you say, Bun?'

'Um, well, maybe.' Bun looked less than keen. 'Why don't you and Nita go? I've got rather a lot of things to do here.'

'Like?'

'Like, eh, keeping an eye on the Queen…'

'While she sleeps?' asked Nita, frowning.

'While she sleeps, yes, and, eh, um…'

'Eating apple pie and hiding under tables?' said Nita. 'You're coming with us, Bun, whether you like it or not! We need someone who knows their way round here, and that's you. And I'll tell you who else we need,' she added. 'That Dunk character. The one who paralysed Jimmy.'

'No!' cried Jimmy. 'I don't ever want to see him again, he's so green and crazy!'

'Exactly,' said Nita. 'Just like the NetherWorlders. If we lurk in the background and let Dunk do the talking, people will think he's one of them.'

'Maybe you're right,' said Jimmy. 'But won't he just mess things up, like he did with us?'

'I think we've got to take that risk,' said Nita.

Late that night, four figures crept out of the castle. They snuck down the hill, bent almost double, running between trees, crouching behind walls, till they got to a barn, where they disappeared from view. Suddenly the back door of the barn opened, and out came four bicycles, visible only by their lights, which could only just be seen as they bounced down the lane, over the rocks and along the stony track to the pitch-dark forest.

Through the forest went the fearless four (well, the fearless three plus Bun), till they came to a marsh.

'I'm tired!' cried Jimmy. He'd never cycled so far and so hard in his life.

'Keep going!' yelled Bun. 'If you stop here you'll sink into the mud and never get out again.'

So they carried on and they carried on, and when they got to the other side, they stopped for a break.

'Are you sure we're going the right way, Bun?' asked Nita. 'I didn't realise it would be so far.'

'Oh yes,' answered Bun. 'This is right, isn't it, Dunk?'

'Mmmm,' said Dunk, glumly. 'The only way there, the only way back.'

'Have you been here before, by any chance, Dunk?' asked Nita. She had a sneaky feeling there was something he hadn't told them.

'I have.' Dunk frowned. 'I was sent to the NetherWorld when I was younger.'

'Is that why you're a bit green around the gills, like those nasty NetherWorlders who attacked Queen Alisha?'

'I'm afraid so,' said Dunk, blushing. And only managing to turn even greener. 'It's the bad diet there, and the lack of daylight. The longer you're there, the greener you get.'

'Tell them why you were sent there,' said Bun, smirking.

Dunk scowled at him. 'It was a punishment. Because I'd been naughty.'

'Only naughty?' prompted Bun.

'Puncturing bike wheels. Stealing things. Queen Alisha sent me into exile, but it was so horrible there, so cold and wet and scary, that I escaped. I managed to make my way back to the castle, and begged her to let me stay, as one of her guards. I swore I'd never be bad again.'

'She sent him to evening classes,' Bun told them, smiling. 'In keeping out of trouble. In being nice to people.'

'I swore I'd never go to the NetherWorld again,' said Dunk, unhappily. 'But I swore I'd do anything the Queen asked me, as well.'

'Oh dear,' said Nita. 'And now she wants you to go back.'

'Yes, but it's only to do a bit of spying, isn't it?' said Dunk, trying to cheer himself up. 'It's not so bad. And we won't be there long, will we?'

'I hope not,' replied Nita. 'So how come you know the way as well, Bun?' she asked, turning to our little friend. 'Were you a troublemaker in your youth, too?'

'Certainly not!' said Bun. 'I've always been very well-behaved, I have. No, I used to be one of the Queen's guards. It was our job to make sure the troublemakers got to the NetherWorld safely and didn't escape on the way.'

'So you've both been there before,' said Nita. 'That's great.'

They carried on and they carried on, up a hill and up a hill till Dunk clambered down off his bike.

'We'd better walk from here,' he whispered. And he led them through the trees, until they could see a village far below them.

'That's NetherEdge,' he told them, 'the first place you get to when you're going into exile. Do we have to go there? Do we really have to?'

6

HARANGA, THE HORRIBLE

NetherEdge stank. It stank of toilets and it stank of fear.

And everything was grey. Not the mad jumble of colours Nita and Jimmy had been so surprised by on the other side of the border. No, here there was a complete lack of colour, a hundred shades of dull nothingness.

The first thing Nita and Jimmy did when they arrived in the town was to hunch themselves down inside their hoods, in the hope that no one would notice they were human. Bun did too, in case his lack of greenness drew anyone's attention, and then they went looking for a place to stay.

They tried everywhere, but all the owners

turned them away without a word. They ended up in a hostelry that wild dogs wouldn't have paid to sleep in. It was disgusting, but they left their bags there anyway, because they knew they wouldn't find anywhere else.

'There's something funny going on,' said Nita, as they went back out on to the deserted street. 'How come all the lodging houses are full, and yet there's no one around?'

An old woman, almost hidden in her shawl, suddenly appeared out of a narrow passage.

She gave the other three a suspicious look but turned to Dunk. 'Are you here for the meeting?' she asked, hardly breaking stride. She was obviously in quite a hurry.

'Oh, yes,' replied Dunk, thinking on his feet. It seemed like the safest answer, the one least likely to identify him as an outlander. 'Where's it happening?'

'In the inn up at the end of town,' said the woman in the shawl. 'You're late.'

So they followed their informant to the inn and went in. The watchman on the door, a great ugly lump of a thing, gave Dunk a dirty look, but Dunk threw him back an even dirtier one. The guard, surprised, stepped aside and let Dunk in, while Bun, Jimmy and Nita snuck in behind him, before the guard got a good look at them.

The place was packed. There was a sea of people and a thunder of noise. A young woman, hardly more than a girl, was at the front, trying to quieten everyone down. Eventually she climbed up on a table.

'SILENCE!' she yelled. And, surprisingly, it worked.

'First of all I'd like to welcome all of you who've travelled so far to get here,' she went on.

'That means us,' whispered Jimmy.

'No it doesn't, silly,' hissed Nita. 'She doesn't know anything about us. She means from further out into the NetherWorld.'

'I know many of you don't like coming to NetherEdge,' the girl continued, 'because it reminds you of the land beyond the Marsh. The world you had to leave behind…'

There was a string of mutterings, followed by a string of shushings. Bun and Dunk glanced at each other.

'It was very important, though,' she went on, 'that as many of you as possible came to this meeting, because we need to make a decision.'

'What decision?' whispered Jimmy. Nita gave him a look.

'It's a decision that affects us all.' The girl was getting into her stride. 'A decision that may change our future completely. Whether for better or worse, is for you to decide.'

Suddenly there was a cacophony of crashing and banging from the doorway behind her. All eyes turned to look, and immediately wished they hadn't for they were confronted by a horrendous-looking creature, bent almost double as he forced his way through the low and narrow entrance. Then, as he stretched to his full height, pushing people, chairs and tables out of the way, his appearance stunned everyone in the room. He had the big nose, fleshy ears and protruding eyes of an amadan, but he was three times as large and ten times as ugly as anyone present, all bulging with muscles and with a smell coming off him like he was rotting from the inside out.

A horrified hush fell upon the crowd, broken

only by a few deep moans and the occasional thump as people fainted. For there was no doubt about it – they were in the presence of evil.

Unlike the girl, the monster didn't need to stand on the table.

'I am Haranga!' he roared, great globules of spit flying from his lips. 'Are you with me or against me?'

Silence. Complete, utter, stunned silence.

'I repeat, I am Haranga!' he boomed, even louder, and the sight of his razor-sharp teeth sent many of the onlookers into total panic. 'Are you with me or against me? You have four seconds to decide. Four...three...two...'

Silence. Nothing but the odd whimper.

'One!' yelled Haranga, in total fury. 'So! You are against me!'

He shook his head – and in a high-speed shudder, an unspeakable variety of revoltingness flew from his nose, ears and mouth, splattering everyone to left and right with snot, wax and dribble.

'You will regret this, you and all your ignorant people!' he thundered.

And they did, already they did.

By this time Bun was under a table, eyes closed. But Dunk was hopping mad. He knew he wasn't supposed to draw attention to himself, but for some reason he had this desperate urge to stand up for the poor, oppressed NetherWorlders. He knew what it was like living there, and it was bad enough without having a great bully of a monster threatening you with violence, and drenching you with gunk.

At least Dunk had been allowed back to the other side. At least he'd eventually found the confidence to speak up for himself, even if some people still thought he was a bit of a psycho. But these poor amadans! You could tell they were so downtrodden, so used to having things go against them, that they'd completely lost their spirit. They were frightened to say anything, or do anything in case they made things worse for themselves.

'Wait, Haranga!' cried Dunk, and the monster stopped in his tracks. 'Maybe you'd better stop yelling at us and just tell us what you want. It's hard for us to decide if we're for or against you if we know nothing about you.'

Heads turned to look, to see who dared to stand up to the foul creature. Nita and Jimmy, on either side of Dunk, crouched even further down inside their hoods to avoid being spotted.

But there was no hesitation from Haranga. 'I stand for Domination!' he replied, with a roar. 'I stand for Haranga, Head of the World!'

'Ambitious, isn't he?' muttered Dunk, to his friends, before raising his voice to Haranga again. 'And what do you want from amadans?' he said to the monster.

'Join me, and you will have your land back, the land you once lived in, the land you so richly deserve! But first you must stop all amadans interfering in the affairs of humans!'

'What does that mean?' asked Dunk, frowning.

'Humans are stupid!' roared the monster. 'It is time amadans stopped protecting them from themselves. If humans want to destroy their own world, let them. And then Haranga, with those who have supported him, if any of you are brave enough...' he cast a fierce glance all around the room and people shrank from his gaze, 'will take over there, as well!'

'You're right about humans,' said Dunk, casting a quick glance at Jimmy and Nita before looking away again. 'Their world is a thousand times better than this one, yet they don't seem to value it at all. But how are we supposed to stop the amadans fighting crime, Haranga?' he continued, bravely. 'It's only natural for us to work for what is good. It's in our blood. We've always done it.'

'Where have you been, fool?' bawled the monster. 'Have you not seen how things are changing? Have you not seen how all your young folk are deserting you and coming to my training camp, to learn how to be really truly evil, like me? Then I send them off, not just to annoy the goody-goody amadans and their puny Queen, but to seriously damage and weaken them!'

'So that's where all the young ones are going!' whispered someone next to Nita. 'To Haranga's training camp!'

'And meanwhile,' continued Haranga, 'I am casting a spell on those conceited beings, those so-called 'good' amadans across the border, who think they're so special. I am draining them of their ability to paralyse! They are losing the Stroke!'

Bun gasped. He couldn't help himself.

'And you, Haranga?' asked Dunk, even more bravely. 'What's in it for you?'

'POWER!' roared the monster. 'More power than anyone ever dreamed of. Power over the amadan world, and over the human world, also. I will own! I will rule! I will dominate!'

'Are there any more questions?' asked the young woman who was in charge of the meeting. 'Surely more of you have something to say on a matter of such importance! Surely more of you are willing to stand up and be counted!'

But there was only silence.

Nita felt sorry for this girl. She could tell, watching how she had handled the meeting right from the start, that she was trying as best she could to rally support among her fellow people against Haranga. But she could tell, too, that she was terrified of Haranga – that she wasn't able to come out and actually encourage people to rise up against him for fear of what Haranga might do to her.

'Let us put it to the vote, then,' said the young NetherWorlder. By now the disappointment in her voice was obvious. 'Those in favour of supporting Haranga and going along with his plan, raise your hands in the air.'

A number of hands went up. But slowly, very slowly. And fewer, far fewer, than everyone expected. Haranga scowled, in complete disgust, and people again shrank from his gaze. Then, with a great roar, he raised his fist and crashed it down on the table in front of him. The girl standing on the table wobbled precariously, but managed not to fall off.

'And all those against?' she cried, bravely.

A few hands went up, but even fewer than before. No one dared to object to Haranga while he was glaring at them. They knew what would happen if they did.

'Most of you have not voted, either for or against,' noted the young woman. 'So who is undecided?'

Hands started to go up. At first only a few, and then more and more, until almost all of the people in the room had their arms raised, including our four friends.

'Fools!' Haranga yelled, splattering the crowd with his venom. 'You are stupid, ignorant amadans and you will come to bitterly regret what you have decided today. First, you will lose your young ones, and then you will lose your lives!' And he stormed forward, tossing the cowering amadans to left and right as he went. 'Follow Haranga, those who wish to join me,' he snarled, 'and may the rest of you rot in hell!'

He pushed the burly watchman out of the way and crashed through the swing doors, head first, followed by a handful of young amadans.

7
FLEUR'S STORY

Most of the remaining amadans left in silence, but others stayed to talk to Dunk. To find out who he was. To praise him for standing up to Haranga.

Nita made her way over to the young woman who had chaired the meeting. The girl told Nita her name was Fleur, and that she was the daughter of an amadan who had been sent to the NetherWorld before she was born.

'It must be very hard, living here,' said Nita.

'It's terrible,' said Fleur. 'There's never enough food, and there's no hope for the younger ones. What can they look forward to, in a place such as this?'

'Is that why they attack the Queen's palace?'

'Of course,' answered Fleur. 'You see, they don't understand why they should be punished for things that happened long ago.'

'But I liked the Queen when I met her,' said Nita. 'She doesn't seem the sort to punish people unfairly.'

'Well, she's never bothered to come to see for herself the way we have to live, so we can only assume she's the same as her father, King Oswald, the one who sent our parents here. He was a cruel man, and a weak one, always afraid someone would try to take his crown from him, and so he made up false charges against anyone brave enough, or clever enough, to challenge him.'

'So the NetherWorlders aren't bad at all?' asked Nita.

'Some of them did silly things in their younger days, as everyone does, but none are real criminals. How could we live here together in peace the way that we do, despite the awful conditions, if we were all the evil, violent types they try to make out?'

Nita had no answer.

'We're amadans too, you know,' said Fleur. 'It's not natural for an amadan to be bad. Our role has always been to prevent evil, not to commit it. We all have the power of the Stroke, you know, even in exile, but we were brought up never to even consider using it against our own kind.'

But when Nita told Fleur what had happened to Jimmy, and how the NetherWorlders had frozen him to the spot, Fleur was shocked. 'Your friend Jimmy is a human, of course,' she said, 'but the Stroke has never before been used in attacks on the Queen. It is another sign of the power Haranga has over our young people.'

'Why are they doing it?' asked Nita. 'Why are they so drawn to his evil?'

'Oh, that's what makes me so sad,' said Fleur. 'They hear stories of how much easier and happier life is on the other side, but know they can never live there. So, when someone like Haranga comes along, offering them a share in Power and Domination, is it any wonder so many get caught up in his spell?'

'Fleur…' said Nita, after a while. 'Do you think

you, or one of your people, would come to meet Queen Alisha? To tell her what you've told me?'

'Why?' asked Fleur. 'What difference would it make? She wouldn't believe us.'

'I think she might,' said Nita.

'I couldn't,' replied Fleur, shaking her head. 'I have to stay here, to look for my brother, Jola.' And a tear trickled down her face.

Nita took her hand.

'Since our parents died, Jola and I have lived on our own,' Fleur continued, sniffling. 'When most of the young men he grew up with went off to join Haranga, I tried, I really tried to stop him. But he said there was no future here, especially with all his friends gone, and that I couldn't force him to stay if he didn't want to. So he went. Three weeks ago. And I've heard nothing from him since. I've got to find him before something awful happens. Before it's too late.'

'Is that why you called the meeting?'

'Yes,' said Fleur. 'Many parents felt as I do, that we had to do something, but they were too frightened to act on their own. I knew the only way to get anything done was to bring together as many of us as possible, to create strength in numbers, so that if we tried to face Haranga, he wouldn't be able to single us out.'

'And did they know Haranga would be here at the meeting?'

'Oh no,' Fleur answered. 'No one would have come if they'd known that. Everyone's far too frightened of him. I felt I had to do something to shock them out of their terror.'

'You were brave, Fleur,' Nita told her. 'I really admired the way you stood your ground, when that monster was even thrashing the table you were standing on.'

'I was terrified,' Fleur confessed. 'I thought any minute he was going to kill me, but I was desperate, too. Desperate to let my people see what he was really like. Determined to let them have their say.'

'And they did,' said Nita. 'They showed him what they thought of him.'

'Not really,' said Fleur, sadly. 'Everyone was so shocked at the sight of him that no one said a thing. And when they had a chance to vote, they weren't even brave enough to stand against him. He came, he walked freely away, and he took even more of our young with him.'

Nita saw Jimmy coming over and suddenly knew what she had to say. 'Right,' she said, decisively. 'Here's what we'll do, Fleur. First we'll help you get Jola back from the monster, and then we'll go and see the Queen. OK?'

'It won't be easy,' answered Fleur, unconvinced. 'Once Haranga gets his claws into someone, he never lets go. Not a single youngster who's gone off with him has ever come back.'

'Maybe not,' said Nita. 'But we'll do our best, won't we, Jimmy?'

Jimmy hadn't a clue what she was talking about but he nodded in agreement. It was always the safest bet.

'Oh yes, Nita,' he said. 'We'll do our best.'

8

OFF TO MEET THE MONSTER

They cancelled their booking at the smelly hostelry and moved into Fleur's house for the night. Jimmy, Bun and Dunk shared Jola's room, and Fleur and Nita shared the other. It was a bit of a squash, but better than sleeping in a toilet. And a whole lot better than waking in the middle of the night to find your toes being nibbled by rats.

The next morning saw a flurry of planning and preparation. Over barmcakes and eggs, Fleur begged to go with them to rescue Jola. At first everyone said they didn't think it was such a good idea, she'd done enough already, but Fleur turned out to be just as bad as Nita at never taking no for an answer. Eventually she wore them all down with her determination and her delicious barmcakes, and they reluctantly agreed.

So there they were. Five against the monster. One not-too-brainy action man, one next-door clever-clogs, one scaredy-ba amadan, one psycho headbanger and one brave and determined NetherWorlder.

And all they had to do was track down the fiercest, nastiest, most blood-curdling monster you've ever imagined (Haranga) and ask him politely to return one relatively harmless but over-easily-influenced younger brother (Jola), and possibly to convince said monster (Haranga, again) that the nasty way wasn't always the best and that if he, by any chance, might consider turning over a shiny new leaf and becoming a model citizen, a friendly sort of overgrown teddy bear, helping old ladies across the road and delivering meals-on-wheels to hungry hedgehogs, then life would be infinitely better for all concerned.

'Rightie-o,' said Jimmy, wiping the last of the maple syrup from his sticky lips and turning to Fleur. 'So where do we find them, your brother and this Haranga?'

'That's the trouble,' said Fleur. 'Nobody knows. People think they're holed up somewhere in the mountains, but nobody's gone looking. They wouldn't dare.'

'I know how to find them,' said Nita, invisible bells on invisible thinking cap soundly jingling. 'We follow his footprints.'

'That'd be fine if we could find any,' replied Dunk.

'Oh, don't be so glum, Dunk,' said Nita. 'Just think. He's at least three times as big as anyone else round here, and the whole place is nothing but one great mud bath. There's bound to be footprints, aren't there, Fleur?'

'I suppose so.' Fleur nodded.

'So we pick up his trail and we find him,' continued Nita. 'No problem.'

'It's what comes next is the problem,' muttered Bun, who was beginning to wish himself safely under the tablecloth at the palace again. But nobody heard him, or if they did they chose to ignore it.

So they did as Nita suggested. They returned to the inn, where the meeting had been held the night before, and scrabbled around in the mud till they picked up the first print. Right outside the building wasn't too good, because so many people had poured out after Haranga, but once they checked the main street, where luckily it hadn't rained overnight, they soon picked up his trail.

In fact, once they recognised the first footprint, they couldn't understand how they'd missed them. The monster had stomped off in such a fury that he'd made deep craters all the way up the road. He'd bashed and crashed his way out of town, and all his young copycat henchmen had trashed and thrashed their way after him, so it was easy enough to follow their path by looking for flattened fenceposts, torn-up trees and battered houses.

The path led across fields to the foothills of the Great Mountain. Up the track went our fearless fivesome (well, our fearless foursome plus Bun), past deserted farms, through a deep, dark wood, until they got to a shadowy lake.

'There are caves on the other side,' said Fleur, pointing across the water. 'I think they're probably camped out in there.'

But they weren't. Or at least *some* of them

weren't. They were lined up on the rocks above them! And with a triumphant yell, Haranga's tearaways lobbed a great pile of stones down on our heroes.

'Run!' cried Dunk, and they high-tailed it down the path and back into the safety of the woods, where they gathered to assess the damage. And it was only then that they realised that Jimmy wasn't with them.

'Where is he?' asked Nita, worried for her friend. But no one knew.

Dunk volunteered to sneak back up the track to see if he could find Jimmy, and the others sat around, biting their fingernails, until he returned some time later.

'No sign, I'm afraid,' he reported gloomily. 'So, unless he managed to crawl off and hide somewhere, I'd say he's been captured by Haranga's henchmen and dragged off to their cave.'

'That's *two* hot-headed boys we've got to rescue now, instead of one,' said Fleur. 'We're not making a lot of progress. So what do we do now?'

'We slow down,' suggested Nita. 'We stop taking stupid risks, and we cover for one another.

Right, Dunk?' She glowered at him.

'What are you looking at me like that for?' asked Dunk, aggrieved.

'Now that Jimmy's disappeared, you're the one who's the most likely to do something stupid,' said Nita, in a bad mood with everyone because she was so worried about her friend. 'Bun's too timid to do anything, aren't you, Bun?'

Bun blushed.

'And Fleur and I are too sensible.'

'I'm not sure I go along with all this boys-are-daft-and-girls-are-sensible thing,' said Dunk. 'Sounds a bit sexist to me.'

'Oh, not ALL boys are daft,' said Nita, nodding. 'Just you and Jimmy…'

'And my brother Jola and most of his friends…' added Fleur.

'And not all girls are sensible,' insisted Dunk.

'Just me,' said Nita.

'And me,' added Fleur.

'Hmmm,' hmmmed Dunk.

And Bun said nothing.

9

JIMMY IN THE PIT

Poor Jimmy lay at the bottom of a hole, where he was woken from a strange and troubled sleep by the sound of a high-pitched squeaking. Rats nibbling his toes? A vampire bat?

Straining his eyes up to the only source of light, high overhead, he saw a wooden bucket slowly descending towards him. When it got level with his head, he peered inside and saw a mug and what looked like a cheese roll.

'Eat, drink and be merry!' cried a jolly voice, echoing down the chamber.

Jimmy drank the contents of the mug in one go and returned it to the bucket, which started rising back up again.

'Hang on!' cried Jimmy. 'I haven't had the food yet.' The bread was stale and the cheese was rancid but he scoffed it down nevertheless. By the time he'd finished chewing, the bucket was gone, the squeaking was over, and it was time to take stock of where he was.

A deep hole – it had taken the bucket over a minute to get back up. A deep *dark* hole – the only light was directly overhead, and it wasn't much of a light, anyway, which made Jimmy think he was probably inside a cave. A deep dark *wet and very cold* hole, at that – Jimmy's clothes were soaking from where he'd been lying on the ground. He had a raging headache, too, like a heavy-metal drumbeat behind his eyes. And when he reached up to try to calm the throbbing, he brushed against his hair and found it was all sticky with blood.

He remembered coming out from the woods with Nita and the others, into the clear light of day. He remembered the view of the lake, opening out in front of him. And he remembered nothing more. He must have been attacked, he decided. From above, probably, by the feel of the pain in his head and arm. By Haranga's boys, presumably, who'd taken him back to their caves and dumped him in the freezehole.

It could be worse, he thought. I mean, if they dropped me down here, all this way, how come I've got nothing worse than a bleeding head, a sore shoulder, a pain in the arm and a raging headache? I mean, basically, how come I'm not splattered on the stones?

He felt around the floor to see if there was anything soft he might have fallen on, like a mattress or something. Nope. Just rocks and mud. Maybe they didn't drop me at all, he thought. Maybe there's a secret door, and they dragged me in here. But no. It was solid stone, the whole way round.

Well, they can't have lowered me down in the bread and water bucket, he thought: it'd never take my weight. So there must be a stronger rope, or a ladder or something. And if there's a way down, there's got to be a way up.

He waited for the next food drop. Waited a long time.

'Mind your head,' said a cheerful voice, and Jimmy

looked up to see the bucket swinging above him.

'You weren't so worried about my head when you were lobbing rocks at it!' he yelled in response.

'Yeah, I'm sorry about that,' said the voice. 'But the boys were under strict orders from Haranga not to let anyone near.'

'I'm bleeding,' cried Jimmy. 'You've got to help me.'

'I can't. The boss'd kill me.'

There was no response.

'But I'll die!' yelled Jimmy. Then he thought he'd try the friendly approach instead. 'What's your name, anyway?' he asked.

'Jola,' said the boy.

'Ah!' Jimmy nodded. 'Fleur's brother.'

'How do you know Fleur?'

'I know her well,' answered Jimmy. 'In fact, she was with me when I was attacked. She could've been killed, you know.'

'I don't believe you! My big sister's got more sense than to come creeping round Haranga's den.'

'She's still close by,' insisted Jimmy. 'And if you

75

want to make sure she doesn't end up with her head split open like me, you'd better get me out of here, quick.'

'But it's too late! Haranga's already gone down to the woods to find them!'

'Then release me, now. We need to get down there and help them.'

'I can't,' said Jola. 'Only Haranga is strong enough to pull anyone up.'

'Get some of your friends and try. If I'm left down here, I'm dead, anyway.'

So Jola went off and came back with four other boys. 'Haranga changed his mind about the prisoner,' Jimmy heard him telling the others. 'He wants the human up here, so we can question him. If he ties the end of the rope around his body, and we all pull, I think we'll manage.'

'It'll only work if he helps us,' said one of the boys.

'I know,' replied Jola, in a fierce whisper. 'I've told him we're going to set him free. He'll do exactly as we ask.'

They untied the bucket, so they'd less weight to pull, and lowered the rope. Jimmy tied it round himself and the four boys started pulling. Every so often, Jimmy would find a ledge to hold his weight, so the boys up above could rest.

It wasn't easy, and it didn't do a lot for Jimmy's raging headache, either. But eventually, after a lot of sweat and not a little blood, they got him out of the hole.

'I'm taking him to Haranga's cave for questioning,' Jola lied to the others. And then he tied Jimmy's hands behind his back and led him away.

As soon as his assistants were out of sight, Jola untied him, and the pair of them rushed off down to the woods.

Suddenly, the fiercest, loudest screech you've ever heard split the silence. It was Haranga, powering through the trees towards them. 'What are you doing, boy?' he yelled at Jola. 'Why have you let my prisoner out?'

Jola and Jimmy thought their number was up, but at that very moment, four arms came swinging out of the trees and lifted them into the cover of leaves. It was Nita and Dunk! They swung the two boys up, up, beyond the reach of Haranga, and off they went, all four of them, into the thickness of leaves, where Fleur was waiting.

10

UNITY IS STRENGTH!

'Jola!'

'Fleur!'

'I thought I'd never see you again!'

And when tears were wept, hugs were hugged, and the two were reconciled (not too easy, at the top of a tree, but needs must), Fleur made Jola promise he would do everything in his power to win the rest of the poor, deluded boys back from the clutches of the evil monster.

And Jola agreed. For, as he told everyone, he had come to realise, the longer he'd spent in Haranga's den, that the haggardly horror cared about one thing and one thing only – himself. That he was seeking Power and Domination for one person only – himself. That he didn't care a bean about the plight of the NetherWorlders, not a single sausage about the future and well-being of the boys who'd given up their families, their homes, everything to follow him, oh no. Haranga the vomit-maker was willing to trample on anyone who got in his way. He was a danger to amadans, to humans, to the whole almighty cosmos, and he must be stopped! Stopped now!

Once the coast was clear, they climbed back down from the trees and joined up with Bun, who didn't have much of a head for heights and had been hiding in a rabbit hole. And when he was told of the plan, he agreed too. Haranga must be stopped. As long as there was a tablecloth or some sort of a hole handy for Bun to hide under or in when the moment of truth came, he'd be right behind them.

'But we need reinforcements,' said Nita, thoughtfully. 'We can't do it all on our own.'

'We could call in the NetherWorlders,' suggested Fleur. 'When we tell them what we're planning, when we give them another chance to stand up for themselves, I'm sure they'll want to help.' She smiled brightly, looking at the others. No one smiled back.

'We'll ask them, for sure,' said Nita, 'but I don't think we'll get very many volunteers. You saw them at the meeting, Fleur. Too many of them have lost hope. They've been treated so badly, for so long, that they've lost the will to fight for their freedom. No, we need to cast the net wider, I think. We need to go further afield.'

'Over the border, you mean?' queried Bun, enthusiastically. 'To Queen Alisha?' Any possibility of going home appealed to Bun.

'Oh, we can't do that,' said Fleur. 'We can't expect NetherWorlders and amadans to join forces. They've been enemies too long. There's too much bitterness. Too little trust.'

'I hear what you say, Fleur,' said Bun, clearing his throat and finding his voice. 'But just because people are different, doesn't mean they can't work together if they have to. I mean, look at us. There's you and Jola – NetherWorlders. There's me – an amadan. And there's Dunk – not quite one, not quite the other.'

Dunk was about to protest, but Nita cut in.

'Exactly, Bun! Exactly what I was saying! And not only have we got NetherWorlders and amadans working together in our excellent little team here, but there's Jimmy and me too, and we're humans.'

'Proof that unity is strength!' cried Jola. 'So, we go out there and reunite the amadans…'

'Defeat Haranga…' added Fleur.

'Sort out the problem of why we're losing the Stroke, while we're at it…' continued Dunk.

'And Bob's your uncle!' declared Bun.

'No, he's not,' said Jimmy. 'But Grandad's my grandad. Now there's a thought…'

'No way, Jimmy MacIver!' said Nita, jumping in. 'I know what you're thinking, and you can stop right now. That grandad of yours is the last person we need around here.'

'But he's cool, my grandad,' said Jimmy, looking round at all the others for support. 'When I was a kid he used to tell me all these stories about how he…'

'And what are you now?' asked Jola. He could be a bit picky sometimes, could Jola.

Jimmy stopped up short. 'What do you mean, what am I now?'

'You said when I was a kid. You're still a kid!'

'I'm not!'

'You are!'

'I'm not!' said Jimmy, scowling. 'Well, I'm a bigger kid than I was then anyway. Are you going to let me get on with what I was saying or not?'

'Ignore him, Jimmy,' Fleur told him. 'Just carry on.'

'OK,' said Jimmy. 'So when I was a kid...a little kid...' he said, scowling at Jola again, 'my grandad used to tell me all these stories of how he'd go round Ireland beating up giants and rescuing princesses and such-like...'

'And you believed him?' asked Fleur, raising her eyebrows.

'Of course I believed him,' said Jimmy, nodding. 'He's my grandad. Grandads don't lie.'

'No, maybe not,' said Nita, not wishing to offend her friend, 'but sometimes they're rather good at making up stories.'

'Stories, lies, what's the difference?' asked Dunk, butting in. 'They're all pretend.'

'Oh, there's a whole world of difference,' said Nita, getting on her high horse. 'Stories are useful and fun, they help us deal with our hopes and our fears. Lies only deceive. They help no one but the liar. Ask Jimmy's dad, next time you see him. He writes stories, or tries to, when he's not piling into the chocolate biscuits. But Jimmy,' she said, looking at her friend, 'your grandad, much as I love him, can't string more than two sentences together most of the time, never mind tell fairy tales, never mind make them come true! I'm not really sure how much help he'd be.'

'But you didn't know him in the old days,' answered Jimmy. He explained to the others that Nita had only moved in next-door since Long-Johns Ilver, Grandad's pet budgie, fell off its perch and got eaten by the cat. 'It set him back something awful. He used to be much more chatty before that. And braver.'

'Yeah, maybe,' said Nita. 'But hardly brave enough to go round beating up giants and rescuing princesses and such.'

'I'm not so sure,' said Dunk, butting in. 'Are we talking about the same old geezer who was screaming and yelling at me in Chapter Two? The one who chucked that horrible sticky stuff all over me?'

'The self-same man,' said Jimmy, laughing. 'Him and his porridge!'

'He's wicked!' cried Dunk. 'Get him over here first thing. He'll scare the pants off that horrible Haranga guy, no problem. Only one thing...'

'What?' asked Jimmy.

'Don't let him loose on me!'

'Grandad's not usually like that, these days, mind you,' said Jimmy, musing. 'Which is why everyone was so surprised. I don't know quite what got into him, really, to make him act so brave. But that's one of the great things about my grandad, see. You never can tell quite what he's going to do next. It'd be great if we could get him over here. He'd be like our secret weapon. Haranga wouldn't stand a chance.'

'Your grandad wouldn't stand a chance, more like,' said Nita, her mind made up. 'A seventy-eight-year-old man up against a horrendous monster? It'd be like putting a goldfish up against a killer whale. A Chihuahua against a Rottweiler. And anyway, what's he on about, saying he used to tackle giants and all that stuff? He was scared stiff at the mention of an amadan!'

'He had a thing about amadans, right enough,' Jimmy agreed. 'But that's because he was brought up to think they were the most dangerous of all. He'd never actually met one, but he believed everything he'd ever been told about them, by his father and his father's father before him. The word was that they'd paralyse you with the Stroke, soon as look at you, and that'd be it, game over.'

'Exactly!' cried Bun, happily. 'That's what we amadans always wanted you humans to think. Our job is to help you, but you were never supposed to realise it. It made our job so much easier, see, if everyone was scared of us, if everyone kept out of our way. Till things started going wrong and we needed your help.'

'And anyway,' said Jimmy, pleading with Nita again. He wasn't used to his best friend going against him. 'Even though Grandad was terrified of amadans, he found the courage to stand up to Dunk, didn't he, like you said?'

'He did indeed,' said Dunk. 'He turned the tables on me, right enough. I was the one who was terrified when he was yelling at me! It nearly did my head in.'

'So, go on, gang,' said Jimmy, looking from one to another. 'Give it a try. We'll see if we can get Grandad here, the lively talkative version, hopefully. And if it doesn't work out, we'll send him back home before he gets into any danger. OK?'

'He'll be in danger as soon as he gets here,' muttered Nita. 'And he'll put us in danger, too.' But she knew she'd lost the argument and, somehow, she didn't mind. In some funny way, she was missing Jimmy's grandad as well. At least he'd be a link with home.

11
ENTER GRANDAD

'But can you do it, Bun?' asked Jimmy. 'Can you open up the SuperHighway, with those extra special powers of yours, for Grandad to get through, even though he can't tell a mouse from a gerbil?'

'I'm not sure,' said Bun. 'I don't think it's really supposed to work that way. Last time we had to do all that business with the badges, remember.'

'Yeah!' cried Jimmy and Nita together. 'Amadansanonymous.com!'

'Still,' Bun went on, 'maybe it'll be easier to get your grandad over. Here's what I suggest…'

So they all listened, and then they did as Bun said. They closed their eyes tight and willed

Jimmy's dad to leave the Great Irish Novel alone for a few minutes.

'Chocolate biscuits! Chocolate biscuits!' they hissed, into the ether.

Then they used the power of positive thought to imagine Grandad wandering into the self-same study that his son, Jimmy's dad, had just vacated, and sitting down in front of the computer. And when they'd done that, they all said, out loud and together, as Bun had instructed:

'Dot dot dot dot, dit dit dit dit, dot dot dot, beep beep beep beep beep, hissssssssssssssssssssssssssssss,' just like they were the Internet connecting.

Somehow something worked, because, unlikely as it sounds, a massive screen appeared out of nowhere, right there in front of them in the forest. But instead of Grandad coming up on the screen, all they could see were some words, slowly becoming visible.

'SORRY, JIMMY,' read the words. 'YOUR GRANDAD CANNOT BE DISPLAYED.'

'It didn't work,' said Bun, disappointed. 'We can't have managed to get him into the room.

We'll have to try again, harder this time.'

So they closed their eyes even tighter, till every single one of them could see Grandad in their mind. Some of them had never even met him, of course, but Jimmy described what he looked like and they did their best to imagine it. An ancient human with false teeth, a grey, pointy face and wispy bits of white hair sticking out of his nose, ears and chin.

Once they'd got a firm fix on him in their minds, they used the power of positive thought to lead him into the room, sit him down in front of the computer, and then they all said together, as though their lives depended on it:

'Dot dot dot dot, dit dit dit dit, dot dot dot, beep beep beep beep beep, hissssssssssssssssssssssssssssss.'

'He's there!' cried Bun. 'I know he's there! Now all together...'

And they all shouted, at the tops of their voices, 'WWWDOTAMADANSANONYMOUS DOTCOM!!'

And he appeared! On the gigantic screen, right there in front of them in the middle of the forest!

Grandad, grinning his toothless, puzzled grin.

'What's going on? I didn't turn that funny television thing on. What's this programme, anyway? Who's that boy? It's Jimmy! Our Jimmy! What's he doing in there?'

'Hello, Grandad,' said Jimmy. 'Great to see you again.'

'What?' cried Grandad. 'He's talking to me! Are you talking to me, Jimmy?'

'I am,' answered Jimmy. 'And I can hear what you're saying, too.'

'Incredible!' exclaimed Grandad. 'Televisions that talk back to you! It's amazing the things they can do, these days. In my day we had to make do with two baked-bean tins and a banana. So, Jimmy...' he said, mightily confused, 'it's good to see you. I was just wondering what you were up to, up in your bedroom. But you're not in your bedroom, are you? You seem to be in some sort of forest.'

'That's right, Grandad,' replied Jimmy. 'I am. And I've got some friends in here with me. Would you like to join us? We're in a spot of bother, and you're just the man to help us.'

'I can vaguely remember you saying something like that before, Jimmy,' said Grandad. 'Or was it your friend Nita? It was a while ago, I think.'

'Not that long,' said Jimmy, grinning. 'Only about five minutes, human time. Fifty pages or so, book time.'

Nita appeared from behind a tree. 'Oh, hello Nita,' said Grandad. 'So you're on the telly too now, are you? I always said you'd go a long way. How are you doing?'

'Very well, thank you, Mr MacIver. Can I introduce my friend, Bunsen Burner, Bun for short, the Queen's official Gatekeeper...?'

Bun took a bow.

'And Duncan Dolittle, known to his friends as Dunk – a reformed headbanger...'

Dunk bowed, too.

'Another friend, Fleur, a fearless NetherWorlder...'

Fleur curtsied.

'And her brave brother, Jola, rescuer of your grandson.'

Jola also bowed.

'We're the team that's going to put the world to rights, aren't we, gang?' said Nita. Everyone agreed. 'Would you like to help us, sir?'

Grandad didn't need long to think about it. 'Fair enough,' he replied. 'For Jimmy's grandad is my name, and putting the world to rights is my very own game! What's the point in living seventy-eight years if you don't use your wisdom and experience to make the world a better place for those who come after you, that's what I say. How do I join you?'

Jimmy told him.

Grandad squinted at the computer. 'So, do you really mean I can climb into this here television thing and come out right beside you, wherever you are?'

'Yes, sir,' said Bun. 'That's exactly what you do.'

'Well, it doesn't seem very likely to me, but I'll give it a go.' Grandad put an arm through and wiggled it about. 'It's gone!' he cried. 'My arm's gone!'

'No, it hasn't,' said Jola. 'It's through here.' And he shook him by the hand. 'Pleased to meet you, sir.'

Grandad laughed. 'It works! Oh well, in for a penny, in for a pound, to coin a phrase.' And he leaned down and pushed his face into the screen – chin, grin and hairy bits.

'That's it, Grandad,' said Jimmy. 'Give us both arms, and we'll haul you through.'

So they pulled and they tugged and, with a mighty schloop, Grandad popped out of the screen, into the NetherWorld. Astonished, he picked himself up off the grass, dusted himself down, looked all around and then proceeded to sing a little song and do a little jig, right there in front of them.

Everyone clapped, and laughed.

'Hey, Grandad,' said Jimmy. 'No limits to the word count any more?'

'Seems not,' replied Grandad, with a giggle. 'Not since I gave that green fellow a severe talking to a while back. Any sign of the rapscallion since?' For his memory of meeting the amadan was starting to come back, now he was in their presence again.

'That was me!' cried Dunk. 'Don't you recognise me?'

'I can't say as I do,' answered Grandad, taking off his specs, giving them a good polish, and then having another stare at him. 'You look much more presentable than that horrible thing I saw before.'

Dunk didn't know whether to be pleased or annoyed, but Nita jumped in before he'd time to make up his mind.

'That's because Dunk's become a real hero since you saw him last,' she said. 'We're in the middle of a quest to rid the amadan world of the worst monster it's ever known, and Dunk here is the bravest, strongest fighter you're ever likely to meet.'

'Well,' said Grandad, shaking Dunk by the hand. 'I'm sorry if I got the wrong impression about you last time, young fellow. I'm delighted to make your acquaintance. Any friend of Nita's and Jimmy's is a friend of mine, even if he is an amadan. But tell me, Nita, what's all this about a horrible monster?'

They explained about Haranga, and a broad grin spread across Grandad's face. 'Ah, this takes me back.' He rubbed his hands together. 'Makes me feel young and vibrant again! You may not believe it, to look at me now, all false teeth and bed pans, but I was the seven-times all-Ireland champion ogrebuster, in my early days. They used to come from all over the country and beyond to ask me to get rid of their nasties.'

'So Jimmy was telling us,' said Nita, not completely convinced. 'That's why we asked you to join us. Are you still up for it, Grandad?'

'But of course, young lady,' replied the old fellow, grinning. 'The only thing I was ever scared of in my life was amadans, and if they're all as pleasant as these ones...' he said, looking round at Bun, Jola and Fleur, who were smiling broadly at him, 'and even that one...' he said, frowning at Dunk, 'then, in the wisdom of my old age, I've become fearless! Completely fearless!'

12

THE SEPTIC SEVEN

Fast forward to NetherEdge, where the Septic Seven rested, had a mighty feast and called a second public meeting.

Grandad came up with the name Septic Seven, by the way, and nobody else was quite sure what it meant. I'm not sure Grandad did either, but it sounded good, like Enid Blyton on garlic, so they all agreed.

'Fellow NetherWorlders!' cried Fleur, on Jola's shoulders, on the table in the inn the following night. 'The time has come for action!'

She told the packed room all about what had happened while they'd been away from NetherEdge and then she introduced each of the team.

'I'm going to take a leaf out of the horrific Haranga's book, and ask you one question and one question only. Are you with us or against us?'

There was no hesitation this time. 'With you!' cried the crowd, to a woman, to a man, to an amadan.

For things had changed. Changed utterly. In Fleur and Jola's absence, everyone had had time to consider Haranga and the misery he was causing. They'd had time to think about their missing boys, and how they were desperate to get them back. They were deeply embarrassed that so few of them had shown enough courage before, when they'd had the chance to tell the brutal eyesore what they really thought of him.

They were impressed by the bravery of the team before them, too, when they heard what Fleur and Jimmy and the others had been through, and this time they were determined to do all they could to help them.

And they were amazed, also, at the sight of NetherWorlders, amadans from across the border, and even humans, joining together to fight a common foe. Never before had such unity, such harmony, such a spirit of co-operation been seen in the benighted NetherWorld.

'Congratulations, my friends!' cried Fleur. 'If we put aside our differences and all stand as one, we can, we will, defeat Haranga!' And her people believed it. For once, they believed it.

'Right, then,' she concluded. 'Some of my gang, the Septic Seven here, will be staying in NetherEdge to help defend us against the enemy and to plan how we rid ourselves of the dreaded Haranga. The others are planning to take a trip across the border, to seek an audience with Queen Alisha herself, to inform her of the situation and to tell her of the threat that hangs over us all. We will request reinforcements and, assuming we convince the Queen that it is in her best interests to support us and that Haranga is a threat to all amadans, not just those in the NetherWorld, then, when they return, we will attack that evil monster and drive him from our land forever!'

A great cheer went up.

'Yes, we will defeat him!' Fleur continued. 'Our sons and brothers will be returned to us, and we will be free!'

'Free!' cried the crowd. 'Free! Free!' Their chant continued as the inn emptied and they returned home to prepare themselves for the hard days ahead. And, despite some nervousness at the prospect of the battle to come, the people of the NetherWorld slept more soundly in their beds than they had for many a long night.

'So,' said Nita, back at Fleur's house after the meeting. 'Who goes, who stays?'

'To see the Queen?' replied Fleur. 'I thought it was going to be you and me, Nita. That's what you said before.'

'I know,' said Nita. 'But I think we should throw it open for discussion. Maybe others have a better reason to go.'

'I'd like to,' suggested Bun, never normally the first to volunteer. 'I want to see my Queen again.'

'OK, Bun,' said Nita, smiling. 'But you can't just run away, you know. You've got to come back here after. You're one of the team, now. We need you.'

'I'd like to go with him.' It was Jola. 'I want to apologise to Queen Alisha for my part in the attacks on her palace.'

'Were you there when Jimmy and the Queen

were injured?' asked Nita, horrified.

Jola nodded, shame-faced. 'I wasn't throwing rocks and I didn't climb the ladder, but yes, I was there.'

'Then it's right that you go. Anyone else?'

'What about me?' tried Jimmy. 'I'd be glad to travel with Jola and Bun. It'd be more fun than just sitting around here, chatting.'

'We're going to be doing a lot more than just chatting!' said Nita. 'But that's fine, Jimmy, you can go, if that's what you want. You know what you've got to do when you get there, don't you?'

'Tell the Queen what's been happening and get her to send reinforcements,' said Jimmy.

'Correct,' said Nita. 'And do you think you'll manage it?'

Jimmy looked at Jola and Jola looked at Bun. They all nodded.

'Good,' said Nita. 'So that's it then, team. Jimmy, Jola and Bun leave for the palace in the morning. And the rest of us plan for battle. Is that OK, Fleur?'

Fleur didn't seem too sure. But she was happy

enough to stay behind and do the thinking. And she was pleased that her brother wanted to apologise to the Queen. So she decided to go along with Nita's trust in them.

'OK,' she said, raising a smile.

'What about me?' asked Grandad. 'You haven't said what you want me to do yet.'

'Oh, we need you here. You're chief porridge-thrower!' answered Nita, smiling. 'I take it you've got some with you?'

Grandad pulled a bowl of congealed gunk out from under his coat, grinning mightily.

13

MEANWHILE HARANGA...

It's time we got to know Haranga a bit better, don't you think? He's not getting a very good press so far.

Well he doesn't deserve it! Because he's the most evil, horrible, frightening, fearsome, shocking, formidable, dreadful, ghastly, gruesome, harrowing, brutal, foul, obscene, appallingly awful creature you could ever imagine!

He's back in his cave, and he's brooding. Dangerously brooding.

'Where is everyone!' he yelled. 'Why is everyone hiding from me?'

It was perfectly obvious why everyone was hiding from him. He was storming around the place like a whale with a pain in its belly, like a bear gone berserk. Bashing and crashing and stomping and cursing like the world's worst nightmare.

'How did that horrible human escape?' Haranga hollered. 'Someone step forward and tell me how my prisoner got away!'

The missing boys, the ones that hadn't managed to slip out of the cave before Haranga had returned, all cowered in the shadows, keeping as far as possible out of their master's way. There was pushing and shoving, shoving and pushing, everyone trying to keep behind everyone else, no one wanting to be the one the monster picked on. But eventually the bravest, knowing it was hopeless and that someone would have to stand up and be counted, ventured forward.

'I'll try and explain, my lord, but don't hurt me,' he begged. 'Please don't hurt me.'

'Then tell me the truth!' Haranga exploded, and the power of his voice made the whole cave shake. Stalactites, formed into ice crystals by thousands of years of dripping, chose that moment to detach themselves from the roof of the cave like an onslaught of frozen arrows. One landed, kerplunk, on Haranga's head, causing a fearful-looking, purple-throbbing bruise, and another scooted down the back of his neck, got caught up in the matted hair on his shoulders where he couldn't reach to dislodge it, and proceeded to drip freezing water down his back and all around his smelly bits. None of this, as you can imagine, made our anti-hero any more cheerful. Oh no.

'Speak to me, boy!' he snarled, for the poor guard was again struck dumb. The spokesman tried as best he could to summon up the power of speech but there was to be another delay before Haranga could get an answer, for at the sound of the monster's latest screeching a thousand and eight bats, sleeping on the ceiling somewhere towards the back of the cave in the warmer, less icicled part, awoke from their daytime slumbers. They fluttered all around in blind confusion, squeaking their high-pitched squeaks and encircling Haranga's head.

'Get off! Get off!' the monster snapped, raising

his mighty arms and battering the poor things aside.

'The thing that happened, my lord… It's not our fault…' pleaded the boy, finding his words at last. 'It was Jola, the one who was feeding the prisoner. Somehow he must have fallen under the human's spell. Then he tricked us into helping to get the prisoner out of the pit by telling us he was acting under your orders and that you'd said he was to bring him up and interrogate him. But the next thing we knew, they'd gone. We sent out a search party as soon as we realised they were missing, but there was no sign of them anywhere. They'd both completely disappeared.'

'Aaaarrrggghhh!' screamed Haranga, again. 'This time I will not suffer fools and incompetents around me. Take all of those who helped the prisoner escape and put THEM in the freezehole. That'll teach them a lesson they won't forget!'

'But, my lord,' the spokesperson stammered 'that's not fair! They thought they were doing what you wanted. And anyway, you know we cannot lower anyone into the hole by ourselves. Unless you help us, we might drop them. They might die!'

'When did I ever care about what's fair?' roared the monster, storming off. 'What do you think I am, some sort of namby-pamby? I couldn't care less if they died! It's all they deserve, so just do it!' And he looked the boy square in the eyes. 'Do what I tell you, now, or you and all of the others will be down there with them!'

And so it was done. With care, and with sadness, it was done. Four boys, lowered into the freezehole as gently as possible. The others managed to get them down without too much damage, thankfully, but the poor boys faced a horrible prospect. No food, no comfort, no heating, no hope.

Meanwhile Haranga continued to fume. He was furious, not only with everyone around him, but with himself, too. Not only had he failed to capture the rest of the intruders, but somehow he had let Jola and the prisoner slip out, or was it up, from his very grasp. He'd had them within his reach when he'd stumbled across them in the woods, and somehow they'd tricked him, outwitted him. He still didn't know how.

And if there was one thing Haranga hated, it

was being outwitted, being made to feel a fool. Because even though he'd ranted and raged at the boys about how he wouldn't suffer fools and incompetents around him, he knew who the real fool, the real incompetent was in this particular part of the story – himself.

Not that he was the sort to take it out on himself. Oh, no. Bullies never do. They take out their frustrations, their insecurities, on whoever's the nearest. On whoever's the weakest. On whoever's the most sensitive. On whoever they can scare into submission.

'Next time...' he swore, to anyone who could hear. 'Next time, there'll be NO escape!'

14
BACK AT THE PALACE

When Jimmy, Jola and Bun arrived at the gates of the palace, the guards took one look at the NetherWorlder's green skin and arrested all three of them.

'But I'm Bun!' cried Bun. 'I'm Alisha's favourite!'

'I couldn't care if you're the King of the Cosmos,' snarled the guard. 'We're under strict instructions not to let NetherWorlders anywhere near the Queen, after what happened last time. And we've to arrest anyone who's travelling with them.'

And so, much to their disgust, our three friends were thrown in the deepest, darkest dungeon, and had to languish there for an hour and a half until Alisha got word of their arrival.

'Bring them forth!' she demanded, and guards were dispatched to haul them out and up and into the Great Hall. 'Let them explain why they tried to smuggle a green-faced NetherWorlder into my presence!'

'I am very disappointed with you, Bun,' Alisha thundered, as he was brought forward. 'You skulk under a table while I am being attacked, then you disappear for days, and the next thing I hear is that you are caught trying to smuggle one of the enemy into my palace! Surely, Bun, you have not betrayed me? Surely you have not joined up with those who are out to do me harm?'

'And as for you, boy,' she cried, scowling at Jimmy. 'I thought you were going to help me, not join forces with my attackers!'

Bun was dumbstruck to be so falsely accused, but Jimmy was determined to set the record straight.

'You don't understand, Ma'am!' he cried, struggling to throw off the guard who was holding him. 'We went to the NetherWorld in order to help you. We were trying to find out what was going on – to find out why the young people there were attacking you, and why your powers were fading. Jola here...' and he pointed to his friend, tightly held in the grip of the fiercest guard, 'came back with us to apologise for that attack.'

'Yes forgive me, your Highness,' begged Jola desperately, 'for my part in what happened. I was young and ignorant.'

The Queen heard what they were saying, and her anger evaporated. 'You were indeed young and ignorant, boy, and I suspect you still are,' she said to Jola. 'But because you have had the courage to come here and repent, I am willing to consider forgiving you.'

She signalled for the guards to release them and Bun came running towards her. 'Are you better now, Ma'am?' he cried. 'Have you recovered from your injuries?'

'I have,' said Alisha, smiling. 'And I'm all the better for seeing you again, my little scaredy-bun. I couldn't bear to think you might have joined forces with the opposition.'

And then she turned to Jimmy. 'You're the one I have to thank for saving me, young man. And you're also the one I asked to find out why we amadans are losing our powers. Sit down here beside me,' and she patted a cushion on the ground in front of her, 'and tell me how you got on.'

'It's a long story, Ma'am,' warned Jimmy, plumping himself down at her feet.

So Alisha called for tea and drop scones to be brought, while Jimmy told her all about Haranga, the missing boys, the freezehole and just about everything he could think of.

The Queen listened carefully. 'Most interesting,' she said, when he'd finished. 'I'm very sorry I sent you into such danger, young Jimmy. I thought I was only asking you and your friend, Nita, to find things out for me. I had no idea I'd be putting your lives at risk.'

'Don't blame yourself, Ma'am,' said Jimmy, eating the last drop scone. 'It was our decision to follow Haranga to his den, so we're the ones that put ourselves in danger. But anyway, here I am, safe and sound!'

'So what about the business of our powers?' asked Alisha. 'I don't understand how your story ties in with all of that.'

'Oh, that's Haranga, too. He doesn't like the way your people protect humans from crime, so he's using some sort of magic to stop the Stroke. He wants there to be as much crime as possible in the human world, so they're weakened, and then he's planning to stroll in and take over there, too.'

'He is truly evil!' said the Queen, frowning. 'We must do everything in our power to stop him, before it is too late.'

'It's the NetherWorlders who are suffering from him the most,' said Jimmy. 'We really want you to help them, Ma'am. They're not nearly as bad as everyone here thinks they are, and they're desperate for your help, isn't that right, Jola?'

'Yes, my lady,' said Jola. 'My people have asked me to come here to offer you the hand of friendship, and to beg you to come to our aid.'

'Hmmm,' said Alisha, turning to her little friend. 'Tell me, Bun, what do you think of the

NetherWorlders, now that you've been there?'

'Forgive me if you don't like what I have to say, Ma'am,' came the reply, cautious at first, 'but I'd never realised, until I went there this time, that the people in the NetherWorld are our brothers – that they're amadans, just like us.'

'Just like us, Bun?' repeated the Queen, amazed. 'Surely not!'

'Yes, my lady,' answered Bun. 'I used to think they were troublemakers, and deserved everything they got. But I've discovered that they're good people, or as good as most of us anyway, and that it's simply not fair, the way they have to live.'

'Really?' The Queen raised her eyebrows.

'Yes, really, Ma'am,' Bun went on, warming to his theme. 'It's an awful place, and everyone's so poor, and there aren't even any schools for the young ones. So it's not surprising that they used to get so angry with us, and come over here attacking our palace. And it's not surprising, either, that when Haranga turned up, promising to give them power and telling them he'd make things better at last, that some of them believed him.'

The Queen looked rather shocked at how forcefully Bun was speaking, but he was determined to carry on.

'I think we've been very unfair to them over the years, Ma'am,' he carried on. 'I feel really bad about what I used to do, taking people there and banning them from ever coming back. So, from now on, I'm going to do what I can to help them, and I think you should too. What they need right now is for us to send as many of the bravest amadans as we can spare to help them get rid of that evil Haranga forever!' And he sat back down in his chair, exhausted.

'Well done, Bun!' cried Jimmy and Jola, clapping and cheering and banging him on the back for making such a brave speech.

But Queen Alisha put her hand up for them to be quiet. She thought for a moment and then spoke. 'Congratulations, Bun, on finding your courage at last. What you have said, and your two friends before you, has convinced me that we must take on this monster you speak of. He poses a major danger, not just to the NetherWorlders, but to all amadans, and beyond them, all humans. Leave me now, while I decide what to do.'

15
MEANWHILE HARANGA, AGAIN...

Meanwhile, Haranga fretted and fumed, plotted and planned.

'I need more boys!' he yelled, to the dark and empty night. 'More wild and ragged, dangerous boys! Not like these weak-willed, yellow-bellied, ten-a-penny wasters!'

He had originally set up base in the caves outside NetherEdge because it was close to the border and therefore a good position from which to plan his campaign, not just against the NetherWorlders but against the amadans as well. But by now he was fed up with the boys he had recruited. They were too stupid, too weak, too fond of their homes and their darling mummies.

Maybe if he went deeper into the NetherWorld he would find wilder, rougher recruits.

So off he trekked, into the very depths of the forest where strangers never ventured, to sniff out the wildest, roughest element he could find. The sort who'd had to scrape a living from the bowels of the earth. The sort who had only survived by outwitting nature in the raw, outwilding the wildest of animals and living in the most inhospitable of inhospitable circumstances.

They'd be the boys, all right, if he could find them! They wouldn't let him down, oh no! They wouldn't let his prisoners escape before he'd got every last ounce of information out of them. Certainly not!

Haranga stomped and smashed his way over hills and through forests until he came to the edge of NetherMidden, the deepest, darkest, dankest town in the NetherWorld.

'Come out, you nasty boys!' he yelled, standing on the muddy street, through which flowed an open sewer. 'Come out and join me!'

There was no response. All the doors and windows were shut and bolted. It was like a ghost town. A foul and smelly ghost town.

'Come out, you bold and wonderful boys!' Haranga cried, trying a different tack in case they thought 'nasty boys' was an insult, which it certainly wasn't, in his case. 'Come with me, my magnificent men, and I'll give you a chance to get your own back on everyone who's made you live out your lives in this foul and malodorous place. I promise you Power, and Power I will give you! Power over adults! Power over amadans! Power even over humans!'

But there was no response. Haranga caught a movement out of the corner of his eye, but it was only a rat, scurrying away. And a mangy dog, on the town scrap-heap, eyeing him malevolently. Mind you, the whole town was a dump, basically, so it was a bit hard to tell what was scrap-heap and what wasn't.

Something foul and smelly trailed from the dog's mouth, and it sneaked away into the darkness (the dog, not the something foul and smelly), for fear that Haranga might steal it from him.

Haranga was suddenly furious. He knew the

inhabitants of NetherMidden were there somewhere, behind the shutters or lurking in the woods. But why wouldn't they come out? Why were they so frightened of him? Didn't they realise he was on their side? Didn't they understand what he was offering them?

'This is your last chance!' he roared, to anyone who could hear him. 'I know you're all in there, you lily-livered layabouts, so I'll ask you one question and one question only! Are you with me or against me?'

There was still no response.

'You are against me, then!' railed Haranga, just as he had in NetherEdge. 'And I am against you!' In utter fury, he wrapped his arms around a giant tree, shook it from side to side until he'd torn it out by its roots, and flung it at the ramshackle building that was supposed to be the town hall, which collapsed into a pile of dust.

All day Haranga roared, all day he threatened, all day he took his anger out on poor, defenceless trees, on rotten buildings in decaying towns, all day he bristled and blistered at invisible villagers.

For the word had gone out, round the whole of

the NetherWorld, that Haranga was the epitome of evil, and that even bored young lads in search of adventure and excitement were advised to go nowhere near him if they valued their lives.

By evening, the monster returned to his caves, in the foulest temper you could ever imagine, and what did he find? Nothing.

He called for his guards. Nothing.

He shouted for supper. Nothing.

He searched in the caves, in the forest, the rocks. Nothing, no one, nowhere. Everyone had abandoned and deserted him. Everyone had eventually realised what a nasty, horrible, no-good lump of gristle he really was, and done a bunk.

'Aarrggh!' roared Haranga, in anger and fury, and the whole of the NetherWorld trembled.

'AARRGGH!' yelled Haranga, in wrath and vexation, and the whole of the amadan universe shook.

'AARRGGH!' screamed Haranga, in a passionate rage, and the sound gurgled even through the mysterious channels of the SuperHighway, even as far as the human world, so that Jimmy's dad, in his study, got a vague feeling of unease, somewhere in the depths of his consciousness. He looked up from page seventeen of the Great Irish Novel, shuddered, and went off in search of the ultimate consolation when things were going bad: a new packet of double-thick chocolate-coated biscuits.

Eventually, Haranga discovered the only people that were left in his derelict headquarters. Four boys, at the bottom of the freezehole. With no food, no water, no heating, no hope. Abandoned by their so-called friends, who, as soon as Haranga's back was turned, as soon as he'd gone off into the forests to recruit another batch of assistants for his war of terror, had abandoned camp, abandoned cave, abandoned any plans of World Domination and returned home to their parents. Forgetting, in their haste, the four down the hole.

'Help!' A hoarse and plaintive cry drew Haranga towards them.

'Aha!' he cried. 'My puny prisoners!'

At the sound of the fearsome obnox, the boys, huddling together for warmth, huddled even closer.

'Where are the others?' bellowed Haranga, and his awesome voice magnified as it travelled down the gap so that by the time it reached the boys at the bottom, it sounded like an explosion. As it descended, it dislodged loose stones on the side of the hole and sent them cascading downwards on to the poor, defenceless heads of the prisoners, just to add to their catalogue of woes.

'We don't know where they are, my Lord,' cried the bravest of the four, from beneath the forest of arms they'd raised over their heads. 'We've heard nothing from anyone since you put us down here.'

'We're freezing,' whimpered another.

'And starving,' whispered a third.

'Oh, shut it, you weaklings!' snapped Haranga. 'I couldn't care less about any of you!'

'Please release us, O Mighty One,' begged the strongest. 'It's been bad enough in the day. There's no way we'll survive a night down here without your assistance.'

'Oh, stop whingeing!' Haranga thundered. 'You're all so soft, you stupid amadans! All you ever think about is your stomachs and your beds!'

But the mention of stomachs made Haranga

realise there was an ache in the pit of his very own that only a tasty creature would soothe. And he went off hunting for something good to eat.

When he'd finished (it didn't take long, because he liked his meat raw and bloody), he chucked the scraps down the hole to feed the prisoners and stop all their weeping and wailing.

16

STUCK IN A HOLE, TAKE TWO

The boys who'd escaped from Haranga's lair made it home, where they did the whole fatted-calf, prodigal-son bit – they ate, drank, rested and apologised to their families for going off on such a foolish venture. They'd seen the light, they'd missed their darling mummies and daddies, and they wouldn't be taking up with the nasty piece of work that was Haranga any more, oh no, and was there anything more to eat, please?

So, it was only when a friend of Jola's called Eric was sitting back in the one comfortable armchair in the house, after all the hugs and kisses and the slap-up meal, that he remembered the four boys they'd left behind, down the hole. He tried to put them out of his mind and return to his slumbers, but he couldn't, for he was a young man of sound moral standing, and he knew it'd be wrong to leave the poor, abandoned boys to their fate.

It nagged Eric all the way through his indigestion, till he knew he was going to have to do something. But what? He didn't dare go back to the lion's den to confront Haranga on his own, and he knew he wasn't likely to get many volunteers from the boys who'd been there with him.

When he eventually explained it all to his mother, she mentioned the meeting in the inn at the end of town the other night, and told him about Fleur and her friends. Eric knew Fleur, and knew she was Jola's sister. She was the right person to go and ask for help, Eric decided, and maybe Jola'd be there too.

Eric admired Jola for being the first of the boys to stand up to the evil Haranga. He'd be the perfect person to have with him when he went to rescue the four left behind. So although what Eric needed most was a long, long sleep, he knew his conscience wouldn't let him leave the others at the mercy of the foul and ill-tempered ogre a second longer.

So, he raised himself up from the comfort of his armchair, belched a few times to clear his indigestion, and headed off to find Nita and the gang. It turned out they were only round the corner – still holed up in NetherEdge, at Fleur's house, waiting for Jola and the others to come back from their trip over the border.

'I need your help,' Eric told them, once he'd explained what had happened. 'Haranga will go stark staring mad when he discovers we've gone. He'll take his anger out on the ones we've left behind and something awful will happen.'

'We'll help you in any way you can, won't we, team?' said Fleur, checking with the gang. Everyone nodded. 'Jola's not here at the moment, but I'm sure we'll manage this one without him, as long as we can avoid the dreaded Haranga. So how do we find these friends of yours?'

'I know exactly where they are,' said Eric, 'and I know how to get them out. But we'll have to go now, because I'm not sure they'd survive a night down that hole.'

So they set off, all of them – Nita, Dunk, Fleur, Grandad and Eric, through the woods, past the lake and then, carefully, carefully, ever so quietly, into the cave. There didn't seem to be any sign of the evil Haranga, so Eric ran to the hole.

'Are you still in there, guys?' he whispered. 'It's me, Eric!'

The noise reached down to the bottom, where the boys were in danger of losing consciousness, what with the cold, the fear and the hunger, which Haranga's leftovers hadn't done much to help.

And if you're wondering why they weren't thirsty, too, it's because there was water running constantly down the side of the hole and seeping through the rocks. So they were sitting in a great puddle, basically. OK for drinking, but not much help if you want to stay warm.

'Eric!' came a faint voice in response. 'Is that you? Get us out of here!'

'Where's Haranga?'

'Gone hunting, I think,' came the reply. 'But you'd better be quick. He might come back any time.'

Eric threw down the rope.

'Tell the smallest to come up first,' cried Nita, ever the cleverest.

'Why?' asked Eric.

'Because there's only five of us to pull him, and it's a long way up. When we've got him out, there'll be six.'

'Good thinking,' said Eric, and he passed the instructions down the hole.

The rope was tied around the youngest, weakest of the four, and the remains of the Septic Seven proceeded to haul him up. Grandad was huffing and puffing almost straightaway, but Dunk and the girls gave it their all and soon a bleeding head, followed by a thankful body, appeared out of the hole.

'You saved my life!' gasped the first boy as they untied him. 'It was terrible down there.' And then they threw the rope back down for the next one.

They realised Grandad hadn't any more strength in him, so they sent him to the mouth of the cave to keep an eye out for Haranga, and the boy they'd just rescued took his place hauling the rope.

From then on, each new boy helped with the pulling, so even though they were getting more and more tired up top, they had enough strength behind the rope to get the captives out. They'd got three boys up and were just about to toss the rope back down for the last one when Grandad hissed, 'He's coming! It's Haranga!'

Everyone ran for cover. It was lucky there wasn't a boy halfway up at the time, or he'd have been tomato sauce, splat, at the bottom.

'Still there, my happy campers?' chuckled Haranga, down the hole.

'Still here!' moaned the last remaining boy, and his voice echoed off the walls, bounce, bounce, bounce, so it could easily have been mistaken for four – well, it could if you were a dim bunch of brawn with bad eyesight, anyway.

'Oh goody,' laughed Haranga. 'Warm enough?'

'Yes, thanks,' said the boy in the hole, not wishing to draw too much attention to himself by complaining.

'Are you hungry?'

'I'm fine,' said the boy, using the singular instead of the plural by mistake. Luckily Haranga wasn't too quick on the uptake. 'I mean, we're fine.'

So the monster, reassured once more, went back outside to eat the deer he'd caught in the woods.

Quietly, quietly, ever so quietly, the Septic Seven minus three plus four set about the last stage of the pulling-four-boys-out-of-a-hole challenge. Grandad kept watch, seven people pulled and one rose up, up and away.

Then, while Haranga was still otherwise occupied with the business of stuffing his belly full of Bambi, they snuck round the opposite side of the lake and escaped, dodging between rocks so as not to be seen by the hungry horror and keeping as sure-footed and silent as eight Indian trackers and an Indian tracker's wheezy grandad.

Phew!

17
INTO THE CAVE

And so it was, two days later, that Jimmy, Jola, Bun, Queen Alisha and 243 of her bravest warriors arrived at Fleur's house.

There were introductions all round, slap-up meals, and more prodigal-son stuff for the last of the missing boys who'd deserted Haranga and gone home to their parents while the monster was down in the woods looking for Jola and Jimmy, a bit of campaign planning by the wise ones (Nita, Fleur and Queen Alisha, mainly), puffweed and elderbox in moderation for those who were old enough and partial, followed by a good night's sleep for one and all, anywhere they could find a comfortable place to lay their heads.

And then it was time for the final showdown. Time to confront the evil eyesore.

Up at the crack of dawn, barmcakes and eggs and off. Out of NetherEdge, carrying anything they could find, from axes to pitchforks, from hammers to hoes, to the cheering, the clapping of proud and worried parents. Joined on the march by every single one of the missing boys, who'd heard what was planned and had come to offer their services, determined to extract their revenge.

Over the fields and over some more, to the foothills of the Great Mountain, went our fearless 400 or so (well, our fairly fearless 399 or so plus Bun). Past deserted farms, through the deep, dark wood, until they reached the sad silence of the shadowy lake. Checking out the ridges, just in case Haranga had managed to recruit any replacement boys, and then breaking up into sections. One group to watch the front of the cave from a distance, in case their help should be required; one to wait on either side in case the hideous villain wasn't inside at all and was out in the forest, watching, waiting; and the fourth group, the bravest of all, to go into his lair to confront him.

'Come out, come out, you putrid pustulence!' cried Nita.

'Let's be having you, you beastly butcher!' roared Jimmy.

'Give yourself up, you foul filth!' yelled the bold Queen Alisha.

There was a jumble, a tumble, of sound as their words bounced off the walls of the cave, sucked in and along and down and around. Followed by a long, ominous silence.

And then came a roar, deeper, louder, more frightening than any roar ever heard in the annals of amadans, in the history of humans. A roar of anger, of challenge, of sheer fury. A roar, unmistakably, of a raging, rampaging Haranga.

'I think I'll go and check on the rest of the troops,' whispered Bun, turning to flee.

'Oh no you don't, Bernard,' hissed the Queen, grabbing his coat-tails. 'This is the moment of truth. I want the best at my side.'

'I'm the best?' whispered Bun.

'One of the best,' said the Queen, putting

an arm around his shoulder.

'And me?' asked Dunk.

'You're one of the best, too.' And she beckoned everyone forward.

Bun had the jumps, Dunk had the jitters, Jimmy the willies and Nita the creeps, Eric had flutters and Jola had butterflies, Fleur had the shivers and Grandad the shakes, but nobody wanted to show they were scared. So they followed the Queen with tippy-toe footsteps, forward, forward, into the cave.

One step, two steps. Stop and listen. One step, two steps, stop and listen. One step, two steps...

'STOP!'

And there, before them, was Haranga, chest heaving, hands held high, with a massive rock the size of a house in his mighty and muscle-bound arms.

'Come one step further, and I shall smash this boulder down upon your puny heads!' he roared.

Everyone turned to run, but...

'Oh no, you won't!' yelled the brave Queen Alisha, standing her ground in spite of her fear.

Everyone stopped, and turned, to see what the response would be.

'I most certainly will!' roared the frightful fiend, and everyone turned to run again. Then:

'Oh no, you won't!' yelled Grandad, pushing forward. He was still with them, was Grandad, still fearless. Getting greyer by the minute, of course, but the days of being tongue-tied, the years of being a wimp brought on by the sad demise of Long-Johns Ilver, his dear-departed budgie, were long gone.

'Away and threaten yourself and stop bothering the likes of us!' he roared at Haranga. 'Sure you're not a patch on the hair-raising horrors we had in the old days and you don't scare me, not one little bit!'

This wasn't exactly true, of course, as even in the old days Grandad had never had to deal with anyone quite as awful as Haranga, and right now he was just a teensy bit terrified, as anyone in their right minds would be. But he took a step forward, the monster took a step back in surprise, and everyone cheered at the triumph of age over muscle, bravado over brawn.

'Yes, away back to the hole you crawled out of!' cried Grandad, encouraged by the response. 'For you're nothing but a mighty great bully, and you know what bullies are if no one's scared of them...?' There was a long empty silence. 'They're NOTHING!'

And, with that, Grandad pulled from somewhere concealed upon his person a bowl of freezing cold porridge and flung it high in the air, like a tapioca frisbee. It struck Haranga full on the face, dribbling downwards in great congealed blobs.

'Bleuch!' cried the horrified horror. 'That's disgusting!' And he glowered down at the wizened old fellow, amazed to see such an ancient attacker, incredulous at being splattered with such a weapon of glob.

A murderous look appeared on his face, as though he was about to toss the rock-the-size-of-a-house on to Grandad's poor hairless head, when suddenly Dunk ran out from behind the Queen. He was hopping mad, at the sight of the brazen bully first of all threatening his Queen and then his hero, Jimmy's grandad. Pulling a nutcracker out of his pocket, he gave the horrendous hatefulness a sweet and mighty whack on the knee, at the same time shrieking, 'Paralyse you! Paralyse you!'

And every single amadan heard it and joined in – a great concerted screech from Bun, Alisha, Fleur, Jola, the boys and every one of the guards. 'Paralyse you! Paralyse you!'

And Haranga stopped dead. Like ice, like a statue, like a waxwork dummy. For even though he'd spent the last I-don't-know-how-long using the full force of his magical powers to lessen the power of the Stroke, to weaken it till it had only a shadow of the strength it used to have – even though he'd always assumed that it would be useless against his mass, his malevolence – yes, despite all of that, the sound of almost 400 amadans all shrieking at the same time was enough to put him off his stride. Not paralyse him, exactly. But definitely enough to stop him in his tracks.

'Go for it, Jimmy!' whispered Nita.

'For what?' answered Jimmy, by her side.

Nita pointed, upwards and outwards, towards the middle of the hideous horror. Jimmy followed the line of her finger and a broad grin spread across his face. He pulled his trusty catapult out of his pocket, loaded it up with a large, round stone that was lying on the floor by his feet, stretched back the elastic as far as it would go, and fired. With pinpoint accuracy, the stone hurtled through the air towards the revolting monstrosity, landing him a mighty thwack right between the legs, just where it hurts the most.

'Aarrgghh!' the monster groaned, automatically lowering his hands to cushion and comfort and protect from further attack his injured area, like you do.

Unfortunately he forgot that he was holding a boulder the size of a house above his head. So as Haranga's legs buckled under him and he fell to his knees, moaning, the rock the size of a house got left behind, hovering in the air, directly above him.

18
NO, JIMMY!

And then, much to everyone's astonishment, just when everything looked like it was going to turn out all right, Jimmy darted forward, straight at the monster, straight into the path of the boulder.

'Don't, Jimmy! No!' cried Nita.

And there was a crash. A dreadful, awful, sickening crash as the rock-the-size-of-a-house thumped to the ground, shattering, splattering everything in its path.

Nita screamed and tried to run forward, but Alisha grabbed her by the hand and pulled her away. 'Run!' cried the Queen.

For the impact of the mighty boulder crashing to the floor of the cave from such a height had caused an aftershock that had set the walls all around to rattle and shake and the looser parts of the roof of the cave to split and to sunder. Great slabs of rock were breaking off, all above and around them, and there was a danger, a very real danger, that the whole ceiling might come down about their ears and flatten every one of them.

So they raced for the exit, as best they could in the noise and the dust, until they made it outside, coughing and heaving, puking and wheezing.

'But what about Jimmy?' cried Nita, pointing back into the cave. 'He's still in there...'

And everyone checked and everyone counted and everyone knew that the worst had occurred. There was no Jimmy.

'I don't understand,' sobbed Nita, weeping and wailing and soaking Grandad's shoulder with her tears. 'Why did he throw himself under the rock?'

And she ran back towards the mouth of the cave to try and find a way in. To try and find her best-ever friend, who she feared she'd lost forever.

But before she could get there, Fleur had caught up with her. 'You can't, Nita,' she said, holding her tightly. 'The whole roof might fall in. It's too dangerous.'

'I have to find him, Fleur,' said Nita, sobbing. 'He might be...'

'I know, love,' said Fleur, sadly. 'I know.'

And then, just when it felt that all hope had gone from Nita's world, there came a sound from inside the cave that made everyone's ears rise on stalks. For it wasn't the sound of the last of the great slabs crashing down from above. It wasn't a dull thud as the walls of the cave fell in on themselves. No, it was more like the sound of rocks moving, shifting, as if – no, it couldn't be – as if they were being pushed to one side. By someone. Or something.

'Jimmy? Jimmy? Is that you?' cried Nita, desperately hoping beyond hope that her best-of-all friend might still be alive.

But there was no answer. Not a word.

And then the sounds were louder. Closer. There was more shifting, more sliding, followed by a deep groan, definitely a groan.

Nita tore herself away from Fleur and tried to get nearer, but there was too much dust. She couldn't see, couldn't breathe, and she discovered, when she got as close as she possibly could, that the mouth of the cave was packed full of great slabs of rock that must have fallen from the roof. There was no way in, no way out.

In utter despair, Nita bashed her fists against the enormous slab that was blocking her way, and then slumped to the floor in defeat.

But suddenly she felt something shift. The rock that she was leaning on was beginning to move! Despite her terrible sadness, she knew she had to get out of there, quick, so she forced herself up from the ground and began running back towards Fleur and the others in case the whole thing came crashing down on top of her.

But when she turned to look back, she saw, to her complete astonishment, that the rock at the mouth of the cave was going sideways rather than forward, moving across like a sliding door, and in the darkness behind it, there was something...someone...

Everyone watched, amazed, as a massive figure, caked in dust, appeared out of the murk.

'It's Haranga!' cried Jola, horrified. 'He's still alive!'

And they cowered in shock, every one of them, for fear the rampaging ruffian had come to extract his horrendous revenge.

But as Haranga hobbled forward, out of the dust, coughing and blinking, spitting and spluttering, they slowly, each of them in turn, came to the realisation that he was holding something in his arms. Something small and still and human. It was Jimmy!

'He saved my life,' wheezed the monster, and his voice was so low that it was more like a whisper than the mighty bellow everyone was expecting. So low, in fact, that they all had to edge forward, to hear what he had to say.

'He ran towards me, as the boulder dropped,' Haranga went on, and he carried the unconscious boy forward and laid him gently down on the grass in front of Nita.

'He threw himself at me, knocking me over, out of its path.' And Haranga broke into a fit of prolonged coughing, before he could continue his story. 'If it wasn't for this boy,' he wheezed eventually, and a gigantic tear dripped down his face, 'I'd be...'

And then the last remaining strength of the exhausted enormity gave out and he fell to the ground, broken, bent and bleeding. 'Duhhhhhhhhhh!' he exhaled, and his foul breath enveloped Nita, the Queen and the rest of our craning-forward-to-catch-every-word heroes, in a fog of disgust.

They shrank away in horror, and when the cloud of noxious gas had cleared, when everyone had opened their stinging eyes, uncovered their noses and mouths, moved forward again to see what had become of Haranga, his voice had trailed off into nothingness, the breath had emptied from his cavernous chest, and he was gone.

Yes. All that lay in front of them, almost filling the mouth of the cave, was one expired enormity. Dead, defunct, deceased, by the look of it.

19
YES, JIMMY!

'Jimmy! Wake up, Jimmy!' cried Nita, turning to her friend and wiping the dust from his mouth to see if he was breathing. He was breathing!

'Try these,' said Alisha, stepping forward and producing the little bag of potions that her magical healer had given her before they set off on their journey. She pulled out a bunch of herbs and held them under Jimmy's nose. She propped up his head then, and poured a few drops of the healer-woman's special brew on to his tongue.

Jimmy gulped, and opened his eyes wide. 'Yuk!' he said. 'What was that?'

'Welcome back to the land of the living, Jimmy MacIver,' said the Queen, smiling.

'I thought you were dead,' said Nita, wiping away her tears. 'What on earth made you dive in under that boulder, you mad fool?' She wanted to be furious with Jimmy, wanted to make him realise how stupid he'd been, risking his life for no reason at all. But she couldn't. She was just so glad to see her best friend alive.

'I didn't want Haranga to die,' muttered Jimmy. 'It was me, with my catapult, that made him let go of the rock. I had to do it, to save Grandad, but as soon as I saw the boulder was going to drop directly back down on to the monster, I regretted it. Whatever Haranga's done, however much of a brutal bully he's been, I didn't want to kill him.'

'So you jumped straight at him, knocked him backwards out of the path of the gigantic rock, and it missed both of you by inches!' Nita was angry and proud, all at the same time. 'You're crazy, Jimmy!'

'It definitely missed me,' her friend agreed, 'or I wouldn't be here to tell the tale. But I don't know what happened to Haranga. We fell back, there was this horrendous crash, and then everything went dark.'

'Something must have hit you,' suggested Nita. 'You must have been unconscious.'

'I don't think so,' responded Jimmy. 'I could still hear these bashings and crashings all around.'

'That will have been the roof caving in, then,' said Nita. 'When Haranga's boulder thumped to the ground, it caused the whole cave to shake like an earthquake. Rocks started flying everywhere. We all had to run for it. We had to leave you behind, Jimmy. I'm so sorry.'

'It's OK.' He was getting drowsy again. 'I think Haranga must have rolled over on top of me, to protect me from all the flying rocks. That's why everything went dark. But how is he? He must have taken the full force of the impact. He must be... Don't tell me... Is he...?'

But his questions went unanswered for, at that very moment, the last of Jimmy's strength left him, and he slipped into sleep.

'So Jimmy saved Haranga's life,' muttered Nita to herself, once she'd checked that he was definitely only dozing. 'And then Haranga saved Jimmy's.'

She made sure her friend was comfortable, and

then she turned to the monster, who lay flat out on the grass.

'He's still breathing, too,' said Jola, who'd been keeping an eye on him. 'I know we all thought he was dead, but he's not.'

'I don't know how he managed to survive,' said Nita. 'He must have taken such a battering.'

'He's as strong as an ox,' said Dunk, 'whatever that is. But what do we do about him, now? We can't just leave him here to die.'

'No,' said Nita. 'It wouldn't be right. Not after what he's done for Jimmy.' She looked at Alisha. 'Can we take Haranga back to your castle, my lady? We could keep him under guard, and see if he's changed in any way. Maybe the fact that Jimmy risked his life for him will have made a difference. Maybe he's not really as bad as everyone thinks, deep down. I mean, why would he have saved Jimmy from the rockfall? It's worth a try, isn't it?'

'Hmmm,' said the Queen, considering the idea. If it'd just been up to her, she would have been sorely tempted to call on her guards to finish Haranga off once and for all, after all the trouble he'd caused. But Alisha was torn. Despite wanting to take her revenge, she was much impressed by the charity shown by the two humans, by their ability to forgive, and she was only too aware of the debt she and her people owed them after all the help they'd given. So, after humming and haaing for a few minutes, she eventually decided that it would be only fair to do as they requested.

'Yes, I suppose it's worth a try,' she said, grudgingly.

So they bound Haranga's hands and feet, just in case, and then they cleaned up his wounds and anointed him with potions, before offering him the herbs and the special brew to wake him up.

'Against my better judgement, we're giving you a chance, Haranga,' Alisha told the monster when he came around, groaning. 'You're going to stay in my castle until you recover from your injuries, and while you're there we'll be watching you very, very closely, to see if there's any goodness in you. If there is, then that's excellent. But if there's not,' she warned, in her sternest voice, 'you'll be cast into outer darkness. Agreed?'

Haranga looked at her long and hard. All sorts

of thoughts swirled around in his not-too-brainy and still rather dazed skull. He struggled to sit up, to try and make sense of where he was and what had happened. And then he saw Jimmy.

'Was it you, little fellow?' he whispered, staring at him. 'Was it you who saved me from the mighty boulder?'

Jimmy nodded, and a miraculous smile broke over the gnarled and crusty face of the horrendous horror.

'And then did you roll on top of me, Haranga,' asked Jimmy, 'to stop me being squished by all those massive rocks crashing down all around us?'

And Haranga smiled again, a smile to light up the greyest of days. 'I sure did, little fellow. It was the least I could do, after you'd saved my life.'

Then Haranga turned to the Queen. 'No one's ever saved my life before,' he wheezed. 'In fact, I don't think I can remember anyone ever doing anything nice for me in my whole life.'

'That's hardly surprising,' said Alisha, frowning at him, 'considering the way you treat everyone. So maybe it's time you changed your ways, Haranga. Maybe it's time you realised humans aren't so bad after all, and let us amadans carry on helping them, rather than doing all you can to take away our powers. Maybe, in fact, you should stop messing around with affairs you're too stupid to understand and let things carry on the way they're supposed to, for once.'

'Duhhh,' said Haranga, scratching his head and looking all around him. 'There's a lot to think about.'

'There certainly is,' said the Queen. 'And you'll have lots of time to do it, under armed guard, recovering in my castle. So are you going to come quietly, or do we have to be nasty?'

'I'll come quietly,' Haranga muttered. 'But will this little fellow be around the place to keep me company?' he said, looking at Jimmy hopefully.

'I don't think so, mate,' said Jimmy, smiling. 'Not for a while anyway. It's about time Nita and Grandad and I went back home. I should think they'll be missing us by now.'

But when Jimmy MacIver, Nextdoor Nita and Jimmy's grandad had said their fond goodbyes to all their amadan friends and slipped through the screen, courtesy of Bun, Official Gatekeeper of the SuperHighway, it turned out they'd only been away five minutes and nobody had missed them at all.

Not Jimmy's Dad, not Nita's lot, next-door, no one.

OTHER RED APPLES TO GET YOUR TEETH INTO . . .

£4.99

1 84121 456 6

CHRIS D'LACEY

David soon discovers the dragons
when he moves in with Liz and Lucy. The pottery
models fill up every spare space in the house!

Only when David is given his own special dragon
does he begin to unlock their mysterious secrets
and to discover the fire within.

£4.99

1 84121 539 2

CHRIS D'LACEY

Jason's Aunt Hester is a grouchy old stick.
But a witch? Surely not? But then, why is there
a whole crew of pirates held prisoner in her cellar...?
Aided by Scuttle, the saltiest, smelliest seadog ever,
Jason sets out to solve the mystery and defeat
the evil Skegglewitch.

'Tis a most riotous, rib-tickling romp of a read.'
Buccaneering World

'I be laughing so much I be a-toppling overboard.'
Pirate Times

£4.99

1 84121 456 6

MICHAEL LAWRENCE

Something's after Jiggy McCue! Something big
and angry and invisible. Something which
hisses and flaps and stabs his bum and generally
tries to make his life a misery.
Where did it come from?

Shortlisted for the Blue Peter Book Award

'*Hilarious.*'
Times Educational Supplement

'*Wacky and streetwise.*'
The Bookseller

The Killer Underpants

A Jiggy McCue Story

£4.99

1 84121 713 1

Michael Lawrence

MICHAEL LAWRENCE

The underpants from hell – that's what Jiggy calls them, and not just because they look so gross. No, these pants are vile. And they're in control. Of him. Of his life! Can Jiggy get to the bottom of his problem before it's too late?

Winner of the Stockton Children's book of the Year

£4.99

1 84362 187 8

ANDREW MATTHEWS

Dido Nesbit is no ordinary girl – she's a Light
Witch. But being a modern day witch isn't easy –
not when you've got to juggle magic with
schoolwork, friends and all the usual problems a
girl has to deal with.

There are another two titles in *The Light Witch*
Trilogy to read!

MORE ORCHARD RED APPLES

All priced at £4.99

Orchard Black Apples are available from all good bookshops,
or can be ordered direct from the publisher:
Orchard Books, PO BOX 29, Douglas IM99 1BQ
Credit card orders please telephone 01624 836000
or fax 01624 837033
or visit our Internet site: www.wattspub.co.uk
or e-mail: bookshop@enterprise.net for details.

To order please quote title, author and ISBN
and your full name and address.
Cheques and postal orders should be made payable to 'Bookpost plc.'
Postage and packing is FREE within the UK
(overseas customers should add £1.00 per book)

Prices and availability are subject to change.